Claim

ADDICTED TO YOU #4

K.M. SCOTT

Books by K.M. Scott writing as Gabrielle Bisset

Blood Avenged (Sons of Navarus #1)
Blood Betrayed (Sons of Navarus #2)
Longing (A Sons of Navarus Short Story)
Blood Spirit (Sons of Navarus #3)
The Deepest Cut (A Sons of Navarus Short Story)
Blood Prophecy (Sons of Navarus #4)
Blood Craving (Sons of Navarus #5)
Blood Eclipse (Sons of Navarus #6)
The Sons of Navarus Box Set #1
The Sons of Navarus Box Set #2

Stolen Destiny (Destined Ones Duology #1)
Destiny Redeemed (Destined Ones Duology #2)

Love's Master
Masquerade
The Victorian Erotic Romance Trilogy

Ian and Kristina's love has been tested over and over, but now one final test may be too much for them to overcome.

The only part of his life other than Kristina that meant anything to Ian—his career—lays in shambles. Now he'll have to decide if he can forgive the woman he loves for betraying his most important secret.

Kristina will do whatever it takes to get Ian back, and this time it won't be easy. But their love means too much for her to give up now.

And just when they think they've finally found happiness, their love will be challenged one last time.

Claim was previously published as SILK Volume Four.

CHAPTER ONE

Kristina

I STAND AT Ian's door knocking until my knuckles hurt, but he's gone. I feel it as much as I feel the emptiness inside me from sending text after text and never hearing from him. I've ruined his livelihood, but even more, I've betrayed what we had together. He loved me, and I let that all slip away because I couldn't handle a few weeks of loneliness.

Looking down at my phone, I look for a text from him but see nothing. I have to try again. I can't let this be the end.

Ian, please let me explain. He meant nothing to me. I love you. What we have can't be over. I won't let it be.

I wait for him to reply, to say something even if it's that he hates me and never wants to see me again, but he says nothing. His silence is worse than anything he could possibly say.

*Please answer me. Tell me this isn't the end.
Tell me you can forgive me like I forgave you.
Just say something.*

He doesn't answer and by the time I reach my apartment, I know this time he won't just let me come back. I'm going to have to fight for him.

But I don't know where he is and just as I think I might be able to figure out where he's gone, the thought of him slipping back into his old addictions stops me cold. If he goes back to doing drugs because of what I've done, I'll never be able to forgive myself.

I have to find him before he does anything, but how?

His agent will be able to tell me where he's gone, but all I know about her is her name is Sheila. I flip through the back pages of Caligula's Dream, but all I find is information about Ian's other books. That doesn't help, but maybe I can find something online that will.

I search for any information about Ian Anwell, and the first site that comes up is his website. I've visited it dozens of times and never read anything about his agent, but then again, I wasn't looking either. Clicking on the About Ian page, I read about him growing up in upstate New York, attending Cornell University and majoring in history, and living in New York City.

Nothing about who represents him.

Not knowing what to do next, I google Ian's name along with the name Sheila and hope for something to come up in the search. It's worth a try. Unfortunately, some woman named Sheila Josten seems to have a very unhealthy obsession with the man I love and every link on the first page of search results sends me to her blog where she spends a lot of time talking about Ian's books.

I move to the next page and find more of his scary stalker and her love of all things Ian. Scrolling to the bottom and after reading what could best be described as a love letter from her to him, I finally find a link to an article from The Post mentioning Ian's agent, Sheila Rogers.

After searching for another few minutes, I find a phone number for her, but before I can call her, my phone rings. Excited that Ian might have finally realized we could work this all out, I answer it but it's Cilla, not Ian.

"Sweetie, I'm so sorry. I never meant to hurt you. Sienna told me what happened. I really am sorry."

"How could you do that to me, Cilla? You're supposed to be my friend."

"I didn't think all of this would happen. I swear I didn't."

I try to control my anger at her, but just

hearing her lame excuse makes it rush to the surface. "You didn't think that website would run an article about me cheating on my boyfriend? Are you kidding?"

Cilla's silent for a long moment, and then she quietly says, "No, that I knew. I just didn't realize you cared so much about him. I had no idea you were dating Ian Anwell and no idea that they'd bother with him at all."

"Bother with him? You told them I cheated on him, and then they dug up who he is under a pen name. Do you have any idea how much hurt you've caused?"

"Well, actually it was the other way around, but it doesn't matter now. I'm so sorry, Kristina. I didn't know they would do that. I figured they'd focus on you and then it would die down. You know, like it did with John."

"Like it did with John? I was devastated when I found out he cheated on me with that waitress. You knew that! How many days did I stay locked away in Sienna's house because I was so broken up over that? It didn't just blow over, Cilla. Just because the tabloids stopped talking about it didn't mean it ended for me."

"Oh, honey, I'm so sorry. I just needed money and I didn't know what to do."

"You could have asked me. I would've given

you money. I would have given anything to make sure Ian didn't find out. Now he won't even talk to me and all because you wanted to find a way to get some quick money."

"I'm sorry. I mean that."

"You just don't get it, Cilla. You saying you're sorry doesn't fix anything. Go tell someone who actually believes you."

I can't listen to her weak apologies anymore. Wishing I could slam the phone down and let her hear how furious I am with her, I click END and throw my phone onto my couch. Her I'm sorry's mean nothing to me.

My chest hurts at the thought that Ian is feeling how I felt when I found out John cheated on me. I remember the betrayal hurting so badly that I wasn't sure I could ever trust anyone again. I was ashamed I'd ever believed he could truly love me, and for a long time I didn't think I'd ever be strong enough again to care for someone.

And then I met Ian and for as broken as I was, he showed me I could love again and believe not only in a man but in myself too. Now with my stupid mistake, everything we'd been through and everything we were lay in ruins.

How would I ever convince him that I love him and would do anything to have him back?

First, I had to convince his agent to tell me

where he is. Dialing her number, I get past her assistant, but I can tell by Sheila's tone that she's not a fan of mine after what's happened.

"What can I do for you, Miss Richards?"

"Sheila, I know you saw the whole mess on that website, but I need to find him. I'm worried he's going to fall back into the drugs because of this. I don't want that to happen, and I know you don't want that either."

"I can't help you, Miss Richards. I told Ian to leave the city with you, but clearly he believes that rag like I do. He'll return when all of this dies down. In the meantime, I'll be working to do my best to save whatever's left of his career your foolishness has decimated."

"I swear I didn't tell anyone anything about Ian writing under that pen name. I wouldn't do that to him."

Sheila snorts in disgust. "You'd just cheat on him while he's in the fight of his life to get that heroin monkey off his back."

"I'm not going to deny I made a mistake, but if you'll just tell me where he is, I'll show him that it meant nothing and hopefully stop him before he starts back up on the drugs. Please, I just want a chance to make things right."

I hear nothing for a long time, like she's considering what I said, but her tone remains icy when she finally says, "I can't help you. I just hope Ian isn't so devastated by what you've done that he falls back into his bad habits. He's too talented an author to be sidelined by nonsense like this."

I want to say to her that the love we share isn't nonsense, but what's the use? The only person I need to defend myself to is Ian, and she won't help me find him. She hangs up on me before I can try to convince her again, so I call Joanne. If anyone can help, it's her.

"Kristina, I know I told you more publicity would be a good idea, but I never thought you'd give me something this fantastic. I swear I've gotten more calls and emails about you today than I've gotten for the past nine months."

"Joanne, I need your help finding Ian."

"The boyfriend?"

"Yes. I need to find him. He's left the city because of this mess, and I need to find him."

"Have you tried his agent or publicist? They probably know where he's gone off to."

Sighing in frustration, I explain who his agent is and how she refuses to tell me where he is. I know Joanne well enough to know she'll see this as a challenge, so I exaggerate how Sheila refused to help me and hope my publicist will be able to drag the information out of her.

"Give me a few minutes. I'll find out where your Ian Anwell has run off to. Just promise me if this turns out all happily ever after that you'll be sure to let me coordinate the PR campaign."

"Fine. Just help me find out where he is and I'll promise you anything."

I hang up with her and collapse onto the couch where he and I sat that first night. All I can hope is that Joanne is able to get through to Sheila. Not exactly the most subtle person, I can't imagine how she'll do it.

All I know is if anyone can, Joanne can.

So much has happened since that night Ian and I met and came back here so he could sign my copy of Caligula's Dream. How infatuated I'd been when my manager contacted me to ask if I'd like to meet Ian. To have a New York Times bestseller and one of my favorite authors want to meet me seemed too incredible for words, but he'd assured me the offer was a real one. As I sat there in that booth at Jax's waiting for him to arrive, I hoped he'd see me as intelligent and accomplished like he is. Never in my wildest dreams had I imagined we'd begin a love affair that would change our lives forever.

Now I'd lost him because of my stupid mistake, and I planned to do whatever I needed to bring him back. If Joanne could find out where he went, I'd brave hell, high water, or whatever obstacle the world threw in front of me to get to him.

As I silently promise Ian I'll do everything in my power to get him back, my phone rings. Lunging for it, I grab it from the other end of the couch and see it's Joanne calling back.

"Did you find out where he is?" I blurt out without even saying hello.

"I did. That agent of his wanted to guard the secret like it was gold in Fort Knox, but I can be pretty persuasive when I want to be. You can thank me later. For now, you need to find a way upstate. That's where your boyfriend is hiding out."

"Upstate? Where?" He'd never talked about anywhere upstate, other than where he'd grown up, but none of family still lived there, so I can't imagine where he's gone.

"He's at a cabin he owns in Hunter about two and a half hours north of the city. How are you going to get up there?"

"I don't know, but I have to get there. Text me the address. I have to find a way to get upstate. And Joanne, thanks. I owe you big."

"Damn right you do. I'll send that over right now. Be careful driving up there, Kristina. It's the middle of winter and they get a lot more snow than we do down here."

"I promise I will, but don't worry about me. I'm a Midwest girl born and bred. I learned how to drive in the snow, unlike you city folk. I'll be fine."

I hang up with Joanne feeling better than I have since I woke up next to Ian this morning. Now all I need to do is find a car, and I know just the person to help me.

Quickly I press four on my speed dial. "Sienna, it's Kristina. I need you to let me use your car."

"The Benz?" she asks, not missing a beat. Only Sienna could get a call from someone asking to use her car and not ask why in return.

"No, the Range Rover. I might run into some snow, and I'd rather be safe than sorry."

"Okay, but can I ask where you're going? After the day you've had, I'm worried about you and you asking to take my car makes me wonder what you're up to."

"I found out where Ian is. He's at a cabin he owns upstate, so I'm going up there and I'm not coming back until I've convinced him to forgive me."

Sienna chuckles. "You must be in love, Kristina. I've never heard you so intent and confident."

"I am and I'm not going to let him go without a fight."

"That's my girl! Okay, the Range Rover is yours for as long as you need it. Do you need anything else?"

Packing my suitcase, I throw some clothes in and say, "Nope. I have everything I need now that you're letting me borrow your car. I won't forget this, Sienna."

"It's okay. I'm happy to help since I feel partly to blame for everything that happened. Cilla told me she called you to apologize but you weren't willing to let her off the hook. I don't blame you."

"She ruins my life and now she wants me to be satisfied with her apology because she didn't think it would be that bad. I can't forgive her for telling that website what I did not because it hurt me but because of what Ian's going through."

"I wouldn't forgive her if she did it to me, so you won't hear me telling you to kiss and make up."

I zip my suitcase shut. "She has her money they paid her for the story. That's all she cared about."

"Well, you're going to find Ian and convince him to forgive you, so don't even think about her. When everyone finds out it was her who betrayed you, she won't have a friend in the world. That money better be enough."

I prop my suitcase up against the wall at my front door. "I'm done packing, so I'll be at your place in a little while. Thanks again, Sienna. I don't know what I'd do without you."

"It's no biggie. I'm an incurable romantic. This is just the kind of thing I like to be involved in. I love the idea of you driving up there to win the man you love back. It's like one of your movies."

"Leave it to you to think that," I say with a giggle. "I just hope it works out like that and he lets me in. I'm worried he won't even talk to me after what's happened and I'll be stuck outside in the snow and the cold talking through a closed door trying to convince him to forgive me."

"No way. This has all the hallmarks of a great love story, Kristina. Now go get your man! And I'll be expecting details when all this dies down since you know you can trust me."

"Got it! Thanks again, Sienna. See you in a few."

I PICK UP Sienna's Range Rover at her building and after she wishes me luck, I'm on my way. I have a little over two hours to think of what I want to say to Ian to convince him that I love him and he loves me enough to forgive me.

As I drive north out of the city, I feel like I'm leaving all the madness of this day behind me. The bare trees along the sides of the highway are strangely beautiful and calming in their starkness, and the lightly falling snow makes me think of a snow globe my grandmother gave me when she visited Sea World once when I was a child.

By the time I'm an hour into the drive, the snow begins to fall much harder and faster, covering the roadway. I'm not worried, though. I'd drive through a blizzard for the chance to prove to Ian that I love him and what we have deserves a second chance.

I just hope he feels the same way.

CHAPTER TWO

Ian

T HE CABIN I bought years ago before I even had my first book published gives me a place to hide out while I lick my romantic wounds. I toss my bag onto the bed in the master bedroom and head out to the living room to start a fire. Thankfully, I made the decision to hire a caretaker who's been more than diligent in his job and left me enough firewood for at least a week.

Not that I want to spend much more time than that out here in this winter wonderland. As I sit back and enjoy the fire I've created, I look out the window and see the snow falling again to add to the six or seven inches already on the ground. It would be just my luck to have a blizzard roll in and leave me stranded here in the middle of nowhere.

Or maybe that would be a good thing. Stuck in this place with sketchy internet, at least I wouldn't be able to keep up with the fallout from the All The Dirt article. I know I shouldn't care about what happens to Kristina, but even now after all that's happened, I still love her and wish she was next to me here in front of this roaring fire.

I've left her all alone to deal with the problem. Not exactly the gentlemanly thing to do. As the thought of her being stalked and besieged by those fucking reporters passes through my mind, I feel bad for a moment.

Until I remember she did this to herself.

And to me. Then all I can think is, "Fuck her."

One minute I miss her more than I can bear, and the next I hate her for betraying me. I want to forgive her for sleeping with that guy on set. Maybe I can. We've both done horrible things to one another, and I haven't forgotten that I slept with another woman. I doubt this Gavin guy meant any more to her than the woman I picked up at the bar that night as I tried to do anything to get Kristina off my mind.

It's not the fucking I can't get past. It's the fact that she betrayed me by telling the world I'm T. Anderson. That I can't forgive because it proves I can't trust her with something far more important than sex.

It shows I can't trust her with who I truly am.

God, if I ever needed the feeling of junk coursing through me, it's now. There's a difference between thinking you need it and truly wanting it, though. I could fall back into that life and lose myself again, but that's not what I want anymore. I may feel worse than I thought possible without Kristina, but I don't want heroin.

I can't say the same about scotch, however. Not that drinking myself into oblivion would be frowned upon by Sheila and anyone else worried about me. Funny how being a raging alcoholic is perfectly fine, especially if you're an author. As if doing my best Hemingway impression provides me with some ridiculous writer street cred.

What anyone thinks about me drinking to forget what Kristina did matters not one fuck to me, though. If the fine state of New York believes it all well and good to make alcohol legal, then I'm happy to be its biggest champion.

There will be no prohibition in this cabin. Teetotaling can go fuck itself. I intend on drinking as much as it takes for my mind to finally give up the memory of her betrayal so maybe I can begin living without her in my life. Scotch and I are old friends. I can count on it to do its best.

The rest will be up to me. That's the tricky part because as I sit here now staring into the fire and wishing she was in my arms, I don't want to forget her. Like some sad masochist, I want nothing more than to think about everything she means to me. I want to remember how she tasted and how her body felt next to mine.

I want to remember everything she made me feel for fear that when the memory finally leaves me for good, she'll actually be gone.

Just like everything else I've been addicted to in my life, Kristina brings pain as much as she gives pleasure. And like those other addictions, just the thought of being with her makes me crave her all the more.

I savor the taste of the scotch as it lingers on my tongue before it slides down my throat on its way to polluting my bloodstream. Another three or four glasses and I ought to be blasted enough to at least black out.

The problem is between then and this moment, all my mind is filled with is her.

The center of me feels empty, like part of me is missing, taken away when I left. I breathe in and sense a hollowness inside me and wonder if I'll always feel like this. Never before has the loss of someone from my life made me feel like they'd taken part of me with them.

I need more alcohol. All this fucking introspection can't be any good for me. Closing my eyes, I take another swig and wish for that moment when I black out to come soon.

Unfortunately, my mind wants to flourish on the scotch tonight. I've been betrayed once again by something so dear to me.

Fuck.

Trying to think of something other than the shitstorm my life has turned into, I fail miserably as my mind returns to one idea over and over. Kristina. Jesus Christ, am I ever going to be able to forget her?

I think about the night she cuddled next to me as I read her what I'd written in Silk earlier that day. Her blue eyes filled with awe at the story I told of us, she squeezed my arm whenever I read a part she really liked. The woman who'd begun as just an actress on my television screen who enthralled me listened to my words as if they meant the world to her. I'd never felt more accomplished than I had that night when she smiled up at me as I read her our story.

A little voice inside my head whispers, "She's an actress, Ian. She was acting. You stroked her ego, and they like that. But you were no more special than any other man to her. How could you be? A drug addict who's gotten lucky with a few books?"

I hate that fucking voice. It's like some

demented version of that cricket in that children's cartoons who exists only to ensure I'm miserable.

Shaking my head, I push that motherfucker and his bullshit out of my head. He's wrong. What Kristina and I had was more than some superficial Hollywood actress sleeping away her insecurities in some guy's bed.

We were in love.

Are in love.

Hanging my head, I sigh. Were in love. It's time I admit to myself that whatever we were isn't anymore.

My phone rings to rouse me from this funk I'm quickly slipping into, but for a moment I dread the idea of answering it as I avoid Kristina. Thankfully, Sheila's name appears on the screen, and I answer hoping she's got something good to tell me.

"Ian, are you at the cabin yet?"

"Yeah. Got here a little while ago."

"Good. I think some time away from the hustle and bustle of the city will do you a world of good."

Sheila's all about the good today, it seems.

"Thanks." I know I'm making conversation hard, but I don't have it in me to make small talk at the moment.

"So I'm calling with some fantastic news. Are

you ready for it?"

I chuckle. "I've never been more ready for fantastic news, Sheila. Hit me with it."

"I have been fielding calls and emails all day about Silk! New York wants you back as T. Anderson, Ian. I think this can turn out to be something very successful for you, after all."

"That's great. Really great," I say as I try unsuccessfully to hide my disappointment at hearing her basically say my career as Ian Anwell is over.

"What's wrong? I thought you'd be thrilled to hear this news."

"Nothing. It's great news. I'm sure you're going to get me a fantastic deal."

The phone's silent for a long moment until she quietly says, "Is this about the Marc Antony book?"

"No. Just tired after a long drive up here," I lie. It really isn't the Marc Antony book, though. It's about not being wanted by the business that's loved me as Ian Anwell since my first book.

"Don't worry about that, Ian. I think we just need to give historical readers time to get adjusted to the news of what T. Anderson writes. Believe me, there will be another author who misbehaves sooner than you can say authors behaving badly. I've got at least two authors I'm sure will unwittingly end up helping you by the end of the month."

I know she's trying to help, but even hearing about her hapless newbie authors isn't enough to make me feel good about my historical fiction career being in the shitter.

"Thanks, Sheila. I'm sure it will all work out."

"Maybe my other piece of news will make you feel better. I got a call from someone interested in making Silk into a film."

"Oh yeah?"

"He read the book and thinks it would be a great project for him. That's good news, isn't it?"

"Sure. I'll leave it in your capable hands. You always do a great job for me."

"Oh, Ian. Cheer up. It's not going to be bad forever. You never know what will show up on your doorstep at any time. It might even be something that will turn your whole day around."

I have no idea what she's talking about, but it doesn't matter. Sheila sees herself as my personal cheerleader, and that's just what she's doing. I can't dislike her for that, even though her positive yet cryptic fortune cookie sayings are less than helpful in my current mood.

"Okay. I'll see what I can do about cheering up. Give me a few days and let me know what you hear from those publishers."

"What about the film idea? I think it could be fantastic. There's a huge market for movies like that now."

"Sure. See what he has to say, and I'll think about it."

"I promise we'll make this work, Ian. Just relax up there and let me work my magic. By the time you get back to the city, you'll see it will all be better."

"Thanks, Sheila. I'll talk to you in a few days."

"Take care, Ian, and remember, it's always darkest right before the dawn."

Her attempt at helping me with pithy sayings is only making things worse, but I don't tell her that. Just because I feel like shit doesn't mean I have to make her feel that way too.

"Goodbye, Sheila."

I press END and toss my phone onto the table in front of me as the thought of a Silk movie fills my head. There's only one person in the world who can play Kate Silk. I know that, and there's no way this movie can be made without her.

So it won't be made.

I take a swig of scotch and swallow hard, wishing its effects would settle in already so I could be too fucked up to think about Kristina and how much I want to see her play the role I've written for her.

The role she played in my life for all too brief a time.

Three drinks later and I'm still unable to escape my thoughts as my mind races with what could have beens and doubts about what was. Had it ever been love? Or was all we had physical borne from my obsession with her?

No. We were off the charts great in bed, but we were more than just that. She was more than just my muse. No matter what mistakes we made, we loved each other.

I still love her.

Closing my eyes, I pray for some relief from missing Kristina.

CHAPTER THREE

Kristina

As I turn on to the road the directions say Ian's cabin is on, the sky seems to open up and snow falls like someone in the heavens is dumping the stuff by the truckload. I can't see more than five feet in front of me, and everywhere is pure white. The road underneath the over half foot of snow is filled with ruts and potholes which make driving even more treacherous. One moment the Range Rover is rolling along fine, and the next moment it's all I can do to keep it on the road at all.

I creep along, hoping Sienna's SUV can handle the conditions to get to the top of the hill, and finally I see what looks like a building just as I reach the crest. Leaning forward toward the windshield, I watch as I get closer and see a car parked in front of a cabin. Smoke drifts up toward the sky from the chimney, and I see the yellow glow of a light coming through a window.

My heart leaps in my chest at the thought that I've found him. Slowly, I come to a stop next to a BMW and hope if this isn't where Ian is that the people inside might be willing to help me find him. Blizzard or not, I have to get to him.

I step out of the car into snow deep enough to cover my feet and halfway up my calves. My first thought is to run up to the front door to get out of the cold and wind, but the snow makes that impossible. It's a heavy snow and I can barely walk through it, but finally I make it to the porch. Shivering, I knock on the front door.

As I stand there waiting, I look in through the windows at my eye level and see a blazing fire but no one nearby. Knocking again, I say loudly, "Excuse me. Is anyone there? I'm here from the city and I'm stranded in the snow."

For nearly five minutes I knock, but no one answers. Finally, I hang my head in disappointment and turn to go back to my car, unsure of what to do now. I can't drive in this weather, and I have less than a quarter of a tank of gas left in Sienna's Range Rover. If I have to spend the night huddled up in the driver's seat with the engine running to have heat, I won't last until morning. But what choice do I have?

My foot hits the first snow covered step when I hear, "What are you doing here?"

Ian's voice thrills me, and relief flows through me that I won't have to spend the night freezing cold in the Range Rover. Turning around, I smile as I see him standing in the doorway, but quickly I realize he's nowhere as happy to see me.

"I came to see you, but I got caught in this blizzard. I got here just in time."

"For what?" he asks, glowering down at me like never before.

"May I come in, please? It's freezing out here and my legs are wet and ice cold just from walking from the car."

He narrows his eyes to a nasty squint, and for a few moments, I don't think he's going to let me in. Desperate to get inside the cabin and warm myself in front of the fireplace, I add, "Ian, do you want me to freeze to death out here? I know you hate me now, but even that doesn't make it okay to let me die all alone in a blizzard."

Slowly, he steps back to let me in, and as I walk past him he says in a low voice full of anger, "Just until the snow stops."

I hadn't expected him to be overjoyed to see me, but his frosty reception surprises me. Everything I rehearsed on the drive all the way there flies out of my head as I reel from how unhappy he is to have me in his presence. I'd had all these romantic notions about what would happen, and with just a few words, he's dashed them all to pieces.

Without saying another thing, he closes the front door and walks into the living room to sit in front of the fire. Feeling particularly unwelcome, I begin to strip out of my jacket, boots, and wet clothes, realizing I left my bag in the car. Not wanting to go back out into the storm, I stand at the door in just my sweater and underwear sure I don't know what to do now since he's clearly ignoring me.

"My clothes got wet, so I'm going to just let them dry by the fire," I say in my best chipper voice as I walk in front of him to arrange my pants and socks on the hearth.

He sits silently behind me, and when I turn around, his eyes are closed and his head is back. Has he fallen asleep? Taking a seat on the opposite end of the couch, I rub my blotchy red legs to get the blood flowing so they'll heat up. Never before have I felt so unwanted in his presence.

"This is a nice place," I say feebly, desperate to find a way to get him to talk to me.

It really is a nice cabin. I wouldn't have pictured him as someone who'd own a cabin out here, but like his apartment in the city, it's all modern. No log cabin look with antlers on the walls for him, not surprisingly. Instead, the kitchen has stainless steel appliances with deep brown and cream granite countertops, and the room we're sitting in has walnut hardwood floors and contemporary style furniture.

He doesn't move in response to my statement. All this silence makes me uneasy, which makes me feel like I need to fill the empty space with more talking. I tell him about my ride there and how Sienna's SUV handles well in the snow, except on the road to his cabin, my thoughts drifting into a nervous tangent when he doesn't even open his eyes at my mention of how I worried I might slide off the road and down into the ravine on my way there.

"The fire is very toasty," I mumble, hoping to see some reaction from him before I begin to ramble incoherently again in hopes of getting some response.

But I get nothing but more silence.

Finally, he opens his eyes and stares for a long moment, practically looking through me, before saying, "You shouldn't have come here."

His words aren't exactly what I'd hoped to hear, but at least he's talking.

"I had to, Ian. I couldn't let you think I betrayed you like I know you do."

He narrows his eyes again as the rest of his

face turns stony to match his voice. "You didn't sleep with that guy, Kristina?"

"Yes, but—"

Before I can get the rest of my sentence out, he interrupts me. "So you did betray me."

"You slept with someone else too, but I had to forgive you. Why can't you forgive me?"

His look hardening even more, he says quietly as he stands up from the couch, "When the snow stops, you should leave."

I reach out to grab his arm to stop him, desperate to explain what happened and how much I love him, but at the touch of my hand he lurches his body from my reach and storms away, leaving me there sitting in front of the fire alone. I so want to tell him how sorry I am and how I need him to understand how this all happened, but I can't penetrate the walls he's constructed.

I know I deserve his anger, but I just never expected him to be able to be so cold. The Ian I know and fell in love with wouldn't be able to shut me out when I'm in the same house as him. Thousands of miles away? Yeah. But not with me just feet away from him.

Does he still love me or even care for me? My stomach drops and I feel empty inside as I think this might be the end of us. I can't let what we were—what we still can be—just slip away with him closed off in a room not one hundred feet away while I sit there unable to figure out what the right words are to show him if we can forgive each other, we can overcome this.

As I try to muster up the courage to fight for him, I see a page of notes on the coffee table in front of me. Sitting down, I pick up the sheet of paper and begin to read over what he's written about the film of Silk. His agent is close to sealing the deal for the movie, and in the margin next to where he's written potential actresses for the part of Kate, he's written one name.

Kristina Richards

My eyes fill with tears that after all that's happened between us he still thinks of me as the only actress to play the character he's written so beautifully. I want to believe this means he still cares for me, that we still have a chance to save us.

But when did he write this? It might have been a week ago or six weeks ago. He might have written this while he was in rehab.

While I was busy feeling sorry for myself and selfishly sleeping with another man.

Oh God! I need to find a way to fix the mess I've made. I need to convince him he can believe in me again. But how?

I walk to the room he's hiding in and knock

on the door. Even if he tells me to go away, I have to try.

"Ian, please talk to me."

All I hear is silence from behind the door, but I can't give up.

"I saw what you wrote about the Silk project. You still think I'm the only actress who should play her."

His shoes make a heavy noise on the wood floor as he walks toward the door and stops. I brace myself for his anger when he opens the door, but it remains closed. I know he's standing there just on the other side of it hearing what I say.

Now's the time to make my plea.

"Ian, please listen to me. I'm sorry I slept with Gavin. I should have been thinking of you while you were going through that hell. I know that. I knew that when it happened. Please forgive me."

The door opens and I see the rage in his dark eyes. Swallowing hard, he says, "I can forgive you for that. I don't believe you care about him at all. What I can't forgive you for is betraying me and ruining my career. I trusted you, and you didn't keep our secret."

Everything in his body language screams how he blames me for all that's gone wrong in his life, and for the first time I realize how hurt he is. I didn't betray him as a girlfriend. He thinks I betrayed him as his muse.

I touch his arm and even though he wants to jerk his arm away, he doesn't. Seeing the tiniest chance to get through to him, I plead, "I never told a soul who you were or that Silk was our story. I swear it, Ian."

"You're the only person other than me who knew I was T. Anderson and knew about Silk, Kristina."

"I know, but I never told anyone. I swear. All I told Sienna was that I was dating T. Anderson. That's it. Maybe someone saw us and figured it out."

I knew that made no sense, but how could Cilla have pieced together that Ian and T. Anderson were the same person?

"Kristina, someone would have to know you and I were together. You told your friend and she sold her story to that website."

I lower my gaze and know I have to tell him the whole truth. In a quiet voice, I say, "You're not wrong about me telling Sienna I was dating you, but I swear I only told her I was with T. Anderson. But my other friend overheard me saying that, and it was Cilla who sold the story. All The Dirt must have done some digging and found out."

"How? There was nothing to connect my Ian life with my T. Anderson pen name."

I hate what I have to say now. "I mentioned to Sienna about how I cheated while you were in rehab. Cilla wouldn't have known that part was important, but that could be how that website made the connection. I'm so sorry, Ian. I just felt so terrible about what I'd done and needed to unburden myself. I never meant for any of this to happen."

The frown he's worn since I arrived deepens and his voice falters as he says, "So you told someone about how you fucked another man while I was in rehab and that's how this happened? First you cheat on me and then because you have to make yourself feel better, you ruin my life."

We stand there looking at one another and not saying a word because he's right. Everything that's happened to hurt him is my fault. I can say I'm sorry all I want. It doesn't make up for how much he's lost.

Hanging my head, I nod as he silently closes the door in my face. I have to find some way to fix this.

I slowly walk back to the living room and sit down on the couch again to warm myself in front of the fire. God, if only I hadn't messed everything up. Why did I have to ruin what we had?

I want to remember when we weren't so lost. Before I cheated on him and betrayed his trust. Before the drugs. Before I lied.

Closing my eyes, I think back to the night he asked me to be his muse. How special I felt that night. No one had ever thought so much of me, and now I'd smashed all that to pieces with my foolishness.

If only I hadn't felt so vulnerable and alone that night Gavin came to cheer me up.

So much of Ian and me can be summed up in that tiny phrase. If only. If only I was stronger when he needed my strength the most. If only he hadn't turned to the one thing he loved more than me.

If only what we are wasn't so full of madness.

I know I have no right to expect his forgiveness, but deep in my soul I know I can't give up trying to find some way to convince him that even though our love is crazy and destructive, it's worth fighting for.

He's worth fighting for.

CHAPTER FOUR

Ian

I PACE BACK and forth across the wood plank floor as I listen to Kristina walk out to the living room. Her being here has changed everything I felt about her betrayal. If I'd never seen her again, maybe I could have forgotten her or at least been able to pretend I didn't still love her. Christ, even if I'd had a week alone I might have been able to convince myself I could live without her.

With her here so close, I can't do any of those things.

Like a coward, I remain hidden in this bedroom instead of marching out to where she sits cozy in front of the fireplace because I can't bring myself to send her away and I can't welcome her back with open arms. I want to do both and neither at the same time.

God, I need a fucking drink.

Of course, I can't do that either since the

scotch is out there with her. Fuck. I can't win, can I?

Maybe I can just fall asleep and pretend she isn't out there, close enough that I could just take her in my arms and kiss her the way I always did if I wanted to. Good fucking luck with that, right?

I lie down and close my eyes in the hopes that I can push everything out of my mind and drift off into a dream of a time when my life wasn't this mess. How long had Kristina been so integral to my happiness? Is it possible that it's only a matter of months that I've been so utterly consumed with her?

If only she still brought that same joy to my life that she did in those early days. Now everything I feel for her is tainted with betrayal.

Covering my eyes with my arm, I wish for nothing else but to forget what she's done to ruin what we were so I can return to being madly and completely in love with her. I don't want to hold this anger inside me anymore. I miss her too much and want to go back to the way we were before I chose that poison over her and made it necessary to leave her.

Maybe if I hadn't had to abandon her to go to rehab she wouldn't have felt so lonely that she turned to another man. More mistakes and more regrets borne out of my addiction.

The scent of rosemary and basil drifts into the air around me, and I inhale deeply, enjoying the smell of whatever Kristina is cooking out in the kitchen. She should have left after how I treated her, yet still she's here making this cabin more like a home than it's ever been before.

I look over toward the window and see the blizzard blowing wild outside. Perhaps that's why she stayed. Of course it is. If we were back in the city, she'd be gone and I'd be alone again.

Taking another deep breath of that delicious smell, the truth becomes impossible to avoid. I don't want to be alone again. I want Kristina.

And the only way to make that happen is to forgive her.

I slowly make my way out to the living room and sit down on the couch without saying a word. Busy preparing dinner for us, she doesn't see me at first and I can sneak a look at her without her noticing. In all the time I've known her, I don't think she's ever looked more beautiful than she does standing there at the counter with splotches of flour on her face as she makes some kind of gravy for the pork roast the caretaker had been good enough to leave for me.

She hums a song I don't recognize as I watch her, but she must sense me staring because she looks up and in those beautiful cornflower blue eyes I see the same look of love that's always been there. That her love remains after how terrible I've been to her is a testament to her, not me. I don't deserve it, no matter what she's done.

Before she says anything, I look away toward the fire, ashamed at how I've behaved toward her. Like always, the words I need to express how I feel seem to be ironically lost.

I listen to her as she stirs the gravy and then sets the spoon down on the counter. The sound of her bare feet padding across the wood floor toward where I sit thrills and excites me, even as I pretend not to notice her. I try to focus on the crackling of the fire as it jumps off the log in the fireplace, but the pull of knowing she stands so close distracts me.

Closing my eyes, I wait for her to say the first word so this silence between us can finally end. A minute goes by without her saying a thing, though, and I open my eyes to see her standing in front of me, still only in her sweater and underwear.

"Please speak to me, Ian. I can't stand being trapped here with someone who hates me like you do. I'd leave like you want me to, but I can't yet. I'm trying to make the best of this, even though I know you don't want me here."

Her eyes tell the story of her misery. Looking

up at her, I quietly admit the truth. "I don't hate you, Kristina."

"No, you just don't care about me anymore, which is worse than you hating me. At least if you hated me I could believe you still felt something."

"I care. Even though I've tried hard not to, I can't shake you. I can't shake my addiction to you."

She hangs her head and in a voice barely above a whisper, she says, "You're not addicted to me anymore. If you were, you wouldn't have been able to leave me like you did."

"I am, but like with my other addictions, I can hold out for a little while before the need presses down on me so bad that I can't stay away."

Lifting her gaze to meet mine, she gives me a tentative smile. "Does that mean you can forgive me for ruining your life?"

I reach out and slowly drag my finger down the soft skin of her thigh. "You didn't ruin my life. You are my life. Before I met you, I was merely a drunken author who had nothing in his life but scotch and success that never filled up the emptiness inside. With you, I was finally happy."

Kristina drops to her knees and presses her cheek to my leg. Gazing up at me with tears in her eyes, she says, "Oh, Ian, we can be happy again. I know we've done terrible things to each other, but can't we try again?"

My hand glides through her brown hair, and I revel at its softness. So much like who she truly is. Gentle and kind, she never meant to hurt me. I know that now. I should have always known it.

"Yes," I whisper as I stroke her cheek. "I can't stay away from you, even if I wanted to, Kristina. Of all my addictions, you're the one I can't overcome. The one I don't want to overcome."

For a moment, she stays silent while she stares up at me, and I see the happiness fill her eyes, but then she says, "Ian, I can't tell you how happy I am to hear you want to try again. I know everything went bad because of me, but I swear I never meant all that to happen. I made such a mess of everything because I was selfish. I promise I won't be that way anymore."

"Don't say that. It wasn't all your fault. Come here."

I pull her up to kiss her lips, wishing I could take away all the sadness I hear in her words. Her mouth melds to mine as I give in to what I've wanted more than anything else. More than just my muse, she's my Kristina, the one soul who knows all my secrets and demons and still loves me.

She cradles my face and whispers against my lips, "I've missed you so much. I was worried you'd never speak to me again. I'm so sorry, Ian. I never meant to do anything to hurt you."

Pushing her hair off her face, I look up into her eyes and nod. "I know. I should have never thought you'd hurt me like that. I should have known better. I'm sorry."

Tears roll down over her cheeks, wetting my fingertips, but I receive one of her beautiful smiles. "I worried I'd never hear you say something like that to me, do you know that? Then when you were so cold when you saw me standing there at the door, I was sure everything we were had gone away forever."

"I was a fool, Kristina. I'm sorry. I never should have doubted how much you loved me."

She buries her face in the crook of my neck and wraps her arms around me, holding me tightly as she sobs, "Promise me we can start over and we haven't ruined all that we had. Swear to me it can be great again like it was when we met."

I gently stroke her back and whisper, "We'll be great again, baby. I promise."

Kristina leans back and wipes away her tears. "This is just like that first night after you signed my book. Do you remember?"

"Yeah. I remember when I slid my hands down to your ass and you had nothing but a garter belt on. I nearly exploded out of my pants right then and there."

As I speak, I do just as I did that night and cup her ass in my hands. This time she's got underwear on, but she still excites me as much as she did the first time she was in my arms. My cock aches to be inside her, and when I slide my finger under her silk panties, I feel how wet she already is for me.

Kristina rolls her hips forward to press her needy clit against my hard cock and moans, "You're such a tease, but maybe we should wait until after dinner?"

"No fucking way," I groan as I tear her underwear off with one quick rip. "Dinner can wait. What I want is right here."

My hands squeeze her gorgeous full ass, and I slip a single finger from behind into her slick cunt. Leaning forward, she slowly runs her tongue over the shell of my ear and moans sweetly as I slide another finger in to join the first, fucking her slow and easy with them.

"Ian, I missed you so much. I felt empty when I thought about never seeing you again," she says in a voice filled with desperation.

I know exactly how she feels. Every cell in my body felt that same desperation every minute I was away from her.

Kristina rolls her hips and I curl my fingers to

stroke that spot inside her I know will bring her the ecstasy she so wants and I so want to give her. She leans back with a look of pure pleasure. I watch as she bites her lower lip in that way that never fails to make her look so fucking sexy and say, "Don't think about that. Think about how my fingers feel fucking your snug cunt and how much you want to come."

"I'm so close…right there, Ian," she coos as I increase the speed of my fingers dipping into her wet pussy.

"Come for me, baby. Let me feel your juices cover my fingers."

Pitching forward, she presses her mouth to mine in a kiss while a low, sweet groan escapes from her throat into my mouth. One more thrust of my fingers into her and she comes hard, riding my hand with abandon. I watch in rapt adoration as every inch of her gives into the exquisite sensations coming from her core, loving how expressive she is when we're like this.

Her pleasure is pure and real, and I silently scold that voice inside me for making me question that. When she's with me, there's no acting or pretending.

When she's with me, she's true to her nature and lets me be true to mine.

As her legs cease their trembling from her

orgasm, I slip my fingers out of her. Glistening and drenched with her, they're evidence of the truth that exists between us.

I bring them to my lips and suck them into my mouth, loving the taste of her as it dances across my tongue. Smiling, I tease, "Almost as good as going down on you."

"Almost?" she asks sweetly, still subdued from coming.

"Yeah, almost. I like burying my face in your pussy, but this will do for now."

Pulling her mouth to mine, I snake my tongue past her lips to find her tongue. I want her to taste what I taste when I eat her cunt—the sweetly musky taste of her.

She settles onto my lap and when she leans away from my kiss, smiles as she says, "That's a thing with you, isn't it? You love it when I taste myself on you, don't you?"

I nod. "Yeah. I love how raw and real it is that you don't back away from tasting yourself on my fingers or my cock after I've been inside you. It makes you even sexier, if that's possible."

"I love how you excite all my senses, you know that? I've never been with anyone who thought of taste when it came to making love."

Shrugging at the compliment, I smile. "Maybe it's because I'm an author. We're very much about all the senses. But how could anyone leave taste out of being with someone? The mouth is all about tasting. When I kiss you, I taste your tongue and your lips. When I drag my tongue over your skin, I taste it."

"And when your face is between my legs, you taste me there too," she says in strangely shy way as she traces her finger over my lower lip, exciting me.

"You mean when my tongue is deep in your cunt licking you until you come all over my face?"

I say it that way to see her blush, and she doesn't disappoint. Her cheeks turn a soft pink and her eyes widen just a bit at my words, making my cock stiffen.

Touching her cheek, I say, "I love how you get shy when I talk like that, Kristina."

"No one has ever talked to me like you do, Ian. Everything you say is so perfect. And so sexy. Like when you asked me to be your muse. Nobody else in the world says things like that."

"My muse..." I whisper and look up into those beautiful cornflower blue eyes so gentle and caring. "I love you, Kristina. Whatever this was when we began it and whatever it became, no matter what, I've been in love with you from the moment I laid eyes on you."

She smiles even as tears of happiness fill her

eyes. "I love you, Ian."

For a long moment, I stare up at her just to enjoy the sight of her with me and telling me she loves me. Me. Ian Anwell, recovering heroin addict. Borderline drunk. The man who left her alone to deal with the fallout from that online rag's article like some kind of dick.

Me.

"Is something wrong? Did I say something to upset you?" she asks in that gentle way that's charmed me from the first night.

I shake my head and tell her the truth. "No. I was just thinking how lucky I am that someone like you would even want to meet me for drinks, much less agree to be my muse and fall in love with me. That's all."

Kristina leans forward and presses her cheek to mine as she whispers in my ear, "I'm the lucky one. How many women have their own love story written for them?"

"None more incredible than you," I whisper back to her.

She sits back and gives me a deliciously wicked grin. "Right now, though, I'd much rather live out a far more erotic story with you, Mr. Anderson. What do you say we act out some scenes of our own?"

This is one of the reasons I can't live without

this woman. Sweet and gentle, she also has a sensual side to her I want to satisfy even more than I want to feel satisfaction myself. What we are is rough and jagged, and I wouldn't have it any other way.

CHAPTER FIVE

Kristina

IAN WRAPS HIS arms around me and murmurs in my ear in a voice low and sexy, "Hang on. We need somewhere better than this couch for what I want to do to you."

I weave my fingers together behind his neck and hold on as he walks us to the bedroom. Staring into my eyes, he says, "After I fuck you tonight, you won't be able to think of another man."

He slides his hands down to cup my ass, carefully teasing my pussy with his fingertip and making me want him all the more.

Leaning forward, I drag the tip of my tongue over the shell of his ear and swear the truth. "Never again will I think of another man, Ian. I promise."

Ian closes his fist in my hair and tugs my head back gently. Leveling his dark gaze on mine, he says, "I plan to make sure of that."

His tone is powerful and deep, and my body aches from the sound of his voice as he promises to make me forget every other man on earth. I yearn to feel his hands on my skin and his cock inside me, filling me up like only he can. I want this to be a new beginning for us—a night that will make all the bad that's happened go away so we can be what I know we can be together.

Happy and in love.

Slowly, he lowers me to the bed and then stands there watching me as if my every moment with me enthralls him. His dark gaze travels the length of my body, and I feel its warmth as it finally settles on the space between my legs. He licks his lips and his mouth hitches up into a something like a smile, but there's a hunger in his eyes that tells me there's nothing sweet about what he plans to do with me.

He lightly trails the tip of his forefinger over the delicate skin of my inner thigh, making it quiver with anticipation, but no other part of him touches me, even though I know he sees how much I want more of him. I watch with bated breath as his fingers draw closer to my dripping wet pussy, but he stops before he reaches the evidence of how much my body hungers for his cock.

God, I want to slide my fingers down my

stomach and over my clit. Just one touch. That's all I want.

But I know better.

Ian seems to read my mind and asks, "You're thinking of touching yourself, aren't you, Kristina? You want to rub that gorgeous clit, don't you?"

"Yes," I whimper, desperate to have something touch my clit so swollen with need. His fingers. His cock. His lips and tongue. My finger.

"Open your legs so I can see that pretty cunt," he orders, and I obey, hoping some relief will come soon.

Ian lowers himself to his knees and with his thumbs opens me up so I'm completely on display for him. If I wasn't so turned on, I'd be embarrassed, but I want him too much to care about how I look close up.

"Please put your mouth on me," I beg. "Please, Ian."

"Not yet," he whispers near my skin. "I want to see you touch yourself first."

Surprised at his words, I look down at him between my legs and see a devilish look in his eyes. "I thought you didn't want me to ever do that."

"Are you embarrassed?"

"No. I just thought you didn't like me doing that."

He slowly rubs the pads of his thumbs along the crease of my legs and places a single kiss on my thigh. Looking up at me, he whispers against my skin, "That was before. We're starting over and I want to see you play with yourself. I want to see your fingers make you come while I watch."

I hesitate for a moment, but just the thought of some relief from my need makes his desire to see me masturbate something I want too. My finger quickly finds its way to my drenched pussy, and I eagerly run it over my clit, loving the sensations I'm rewarded with. Every cell in my body feels alive.

Ian watches as I dip my finger into my body and pull it out to return to my clit, coating that incredible bundle of sensitive nerves with my juices. It makes my pussy slick, and my fingers slide through over my wet skin as I begin to play with myself in earnest.

With each pass over my clit, I feel a wave of excitement wash over me as second by second I inch closer to my release. I want to come so fucking badly. Opening my legs as wide as I can, I lift my hips off the bed and rock against my hand, loving how sexy I feel knowing Ian's watching me masturbate.

He says nothing, but I hear him moan low and deep when I arch my back in ecstasy right before I come. I open my eyes for a second to see him watching with rapt attention as my finger goes to town on my clit, and for a moment I wish he'd stop me so his mouth could finish me off, but then I feel my release begin deep inside me and before I know it, my legs go weak and I bury my fingers inside me.

My eyes stay closed through the aftershocks my orgasm gives me, but I feel him move over me. My body lax from coming, I slowly open them to see him smiling down at me with a ravenous look in his eyes.

"You're so fucking beautiful when you let yourself go, you know that?"

"Am I?" I ask shyly, suddenly realizing this is the first time I've ever played with myself in front of any man.

Sucking my finger into his mouth, he flicks his tongue over it. Slowly he pulls back and says, "So fucking sexy. And you taste incredible."

He kisses me and I taste myself on his tongue like he enjoys. Raw and sensual, he groans as he runs his finger across my collarbone and under my sweater to feel the tops of my breasts. "Your cunt is the sexiest shade of pink I've ever seen. I wanted to stop you and bury my face into that pink skin to taste you, but watching you fuck yourself might have been the hottest thing I've ever seen."

I close my eyes when his fingers reach my already tightened nipples and moan as he pinches them. "I'd rather feel you touch me than my fingers, though."

He leans down and says low in my ear, "You want to feel my fingers fuck you, Kristina?"

"No."

"No?" he asks in surprise at my answer.

Opening my eyes, I look into his and know he wants the same thing I want. "No. I want to feel your cock inside me as you fuck me long and slow. Will you fuck me like that, Ian?"

"I'm going to fuck you long and slow, baby. And then hard and fast. I want your body to crave only me from now on. Is that what you want, Kristina?"

I reach down and stroke his long, stiff cock and watch the need fill his eyes. "I want this cock and only this cock. I want to feel it deep inside me as I ride it. I want to feel it fill me up like no man ever has before. That's what I want."

Ian rolls us over so he's beneath me and cups my ass in his hands. His eyes sparkle with desire as he says, "Your wish is my command, my muse. Let me see you ride my cock."

I roll my hips, and he slides through my wet

folds to my entrance. Fisting his hand in my hair, he tugs my mouth down to meet his and lifts his hips off the bed to bury his cock keep inside me in one slow thrust. Each inch feels better than the last until he's fully nested inside my body, the two of us joined in the most intimate way a man and woman can be.

His tongue dances over mine, delivering another level of sensuality to my mouth as he pumps in and out of me and I meet his thrusts with my own, riding him as he commanded. Every inch of my body craves his touch, jealous of my mouth and pussy getting all the attention.

He's everything I've ever wanted in a lover. Powerful, sensual, and focused on my complete pleasure, Ian's my own sex god to this muse.

Gently tugging my head back, he looks into my eyes and whispers in a hoarse voice full of need, "Sit up on me, baby. I want to watch you make love to me."

I feel sexier than I've ever felt with any other man. Other boyfriends made me feel self-conscious and never good enough, but not Ian. When we're together like this, his gaze never leaves me, a sign of his attentiveness and adoration. He looks at me like I truly am worthy of being called a muse, and for that, I love him all the more.

"What are you thinking about?" he asks as I realize I've become lost in my thoughts of how much I adore him.

"You," I say with a smile before he plunges his cock into me once again and hits that spot that makes my eyes want to roll into the back of my head.

He slides his hands up to my hips to control my pace, a sign he's getting close to coming and doesn't want to yet. Staring up at me, he squeezes my flesh and moans, "Slow down. I want to make this last."

I still my movement on top of him, feeling him fill me completely, and flatten my palms against his stomach to balance myself. In his eyes, I see he's working hard to hold back, but I don't want him to stop. I want to feel him explode inside me and watch the ecstasy wash over his features as he comes.

"Let me see you come apart like you love to see in me. I want to see the effect I have on you."

"Most women like a man to go for a long time," he says with a grin that looks so good on him.

Trailing my fingertip over the line of dark hair that leads from his abs to his cock, I say, "I'm not most women. We have all night, so we'll have a long time. I want to see you when I make you come."

He loosens his hold on my hips and licks his lips. "I'm sure I look like any other man, Kristina."

I shake my head, sure he couldn't be more mistaken. "No, I don't believe that. Not someone who's as sensual as you are."

"You've seen me come before."

Leaning down, I kiss his lips softly and whisper, "That was before. Everything is different now between us, isn't it?"

His gaze softens and he nods. "Yeah."

"Then show me what I do to you for the first time again."

Stroking my cheek, he says sweetly, "If that's what you want."

He lifts his hips off the bed to once again begin fucking me, and whatever sweetness that had been present a moment ago disappears as he pulls me hard down on top of him. His kiss nearly takes my breath away, and his moans tell me our lovemaking thrills him as much as it thrills me.

With a hard slap, his hand lands on my ass, sending waves of pain and pleasure racing through me. Surprised, I look down at him, and he says so sexy, "My Kristina likes it rough, doesn't she?"

Sliding up and down his cock quicker now as I inch closer to my orgasm, I moan, "Only with you."

Another hard slap stings the other cheek, and with a grunt, he pushes me hard down onto him. "Good. Now ride me and get me off, baby."

I rock and roll back and forth on him and cup my breasts to keep them from bouncing all over as I ride him with abandon. Just before I reach my climax, he pushes my hands away and sits up to take an excited nipple into his mouth. Sucking hard, he stares up at me as I come, my orgasm intensified by the feeling of his teeth sinking into the tender skin of my breast.

My thighs quiver uncontrollably as wave after wave of ecstasy rolls over me, and the incredible sensations his mouth and cock are giving me blend into a second orgasm that makes everything go dark in front of my eyes. Collapsing on top of him, I groan, "Oh my God, Ian! I've never felt like that."

He still hasn't come, so I know I have to fight the urge to curl up next to him and enjoy the afterglow of mind-blowing sex. Pushing myself back up, I look down into his eyes and see my orgasm has brought him to the brink of release.

"I'm almost there, baby. Just a few more seconds and I'll give you what you want."

My clit, still so sensitive, rubs up against the base of his cock and I feel the beginning of another orgasm start deep inside me. Rocking against him, I slide him over my G-spot and barely hold back coming again because I want to see him come apart under me.

Suddenly, Ian rolls me over onto my back and rears back, sliding his cock out of me until just the head still remains inside my pussy. A look of pure need flashes in his eyes, and for a moment he looks like a man possessed. Then he plunges into me, filling me and touching all the right places with every inch of him.

A long groan escapes his throat, and his cock twitches inside me as I begin to come again. I feel him come just as I do, and then for a long moment it's just the two of us in the world. Those dark eyes fix on me, staring into my soul, and I watch him wince like he's in pain when the last of his release flows into me.

Ian kisses me long and deep before he buries his head in the pillow next to me and whispers, "That was incredible. You're incredible."

I run my fingers down his back and feel the light layer of perspiration covering his smooth skin. I could lay here for the rest of time with him still inside me and me stroking his back as the two of us come down from the best sex we've ever had. This is what love is.

This is what we are.

A CHILL RACES down my back as I lay there in Ian's arms, and I snuggle up to his side to get warm. Wrapping his arm around me, he says, "I think the power went out. The blizzard probably knocked it out, and I don't have a generator."

"Are you trying to find a nice way to say we're going to freeze to death up here in the hinterlands?" I say, half-teasing, half-serious. I love him, but the idea of us dying Romeo and Juliet style in each other's arms as the temperature drops and we freeze solid isn't one I find very appealing.

My attempt at humor makes him chuckle. "No. We have the fire in the living room, so why don't we head out there, but I'm afraid we're going to need clothes for a little while."

We lay there in the dark, not wanting to move from our cozy spot, as I think about what I have to wear since my suitcase is still in the car. My panties sit in a pile of ripped fabric, and my pants are likely still damp from the walk to the cabin through more than half a foot of snow.

At least my sweater is still in one piece. Maybe my top half won't freeze.

"My clothes are all in the suitcase I left in the car," I mumble against his still warm skin. "Other than that, I have a sweater and a pair of pants that are still drying out near the fire."

Ian squeezes me against him and chuckles. "I have blankets. We can make our way out to the fire and curl up in front of it. I can tell you about the news my agent gave me today."

He sounds happy about whatever the news is, so I sit up and tug on his arm. "Okay, let's go. The idea of freezing to death here is getting scarier by the minute."

We walk back out to the living room naked, and sitting on the couch, we cuddle together under a white down comforter Ian grabbed on our way past one of the other bedrooms. The blazing fire instantly warms me, and I turn to see him reaching for the notes I'd read earlier.

"So Sheila called today to let me know someone contacted her about a film of Silk."

His news thrills me. "That's terrific! I think anything you write would be so wonderful as a film."

For a moment, sadness fills his eyes. "Yeah, well, not anything. The Caligula's Dream film doesn't look like it's going to happen now."

"Why?"

"The news about me being T. Anderson and writing something considered erotica made them reconsider, I guess."

I hate that he's suffering because of my stupid mistakes. Pressing my cheek to his chest, I hold him to me. "I'm so sorry, Ian. I'm sorry they did that because of what I did. I never meant for any of that to happen."

His lips gently press against the top of my head in a kiss. "It's okay. What do they say? When one door closes, another one opens? Maybe that's what this Silk film could be."

I look up to see the sadness in his eyes is gone now. "It's so exciting, isn't it? What did your agent say about when it could happen?"

"These things take a while. By the time the actors come in on a project, it's been through so many hoops most don't even make it. But at least there's interest."

"I'm so happy for you, Ian."

"For us," he says as he pulls me into his arms. "Us. It's our story. And Sheila told me she's gotten a lot of interest from New York about publishing the story too."

"That's fantastic!" I say as he hugs me tighter. "At least there's some good coming out of all that awful mess."

Ian remains quiet for a long time, and then says, "I won't give them the rights unless you're Kate Silk. You're the only one who could play her."

Tears well in my eyes as I finally understand how much Silk is our story. Looking up at him, I smile as I begin to cry. "I'd be honored if they'd consider me for the part."

"Not consider. I plan on making that one of the non-negotiable terms of the deal. Unless it's you, I won't do it."

"Why? There are any number of actresses who could do this character justice, and this is a big chance for you. You don't have to make them choose me. It's more than enough of an honor to know that this story is about you and me."

"No. Kristina, it's always been only you. I can't even imagine anyone else playing this part."

I kiss him for being so sweet. "Who do you want for the part of Sean?"

He looks up toward the ceiling and shakes his head. "I hadn't thought about it. I guess I should have since those are going to be some pretty hot scenes."

"I think he'd have to be handsome and sexy," I tease.

"I don't want to think about some sexy handsome guy with you right now," he says, narrowing his eyes to a faux angry squint.

Trying to keep the smile from my face, I say, "Well, I guess you could demand the actor be someone hideous."

"I might want to since Silk and Steel has become far more romantic than erotic."

"Really?"

Ian nods and kisses me. "Love does that to a man."

"I like that. Love does that to a man. So what's going to happen to Kate and Sean?"

"They live happily ever after."

His dark eyes stare into mine as I wonder if that's really possible for us. "Do you think we will?"

"I think this is a whole new beginning for us, so anything's possible. How does happily ever after sound to you?"

Tapping him on the tip of his nose, I smile. "I think it sounds wonderful."

And for the first time in my life, my future with a man looks exactly that. Wonderful. And I wouldn't have it any other way.

CHAPTER SIX

Ian

KRISTINA CURLS UP against me as I tell her everything Sheila said earlier. When I'd first heard about the film and book possibilities, I hadn't cared much, but now as I watch the woman who inspired Silk and my writing, I can't help but be excited about the future, both for my work and Kristina and me.

"Do you think it will be shot in New York? It would be so great to work in the city again," she says as she hugs me.

I stroke her hair and imagine how great it would be to hold her in my arms each night and then watch her work each day. Nothing would make me happier at this moment.

"Maybe it will since it's set in New York. I'll have to see."

"I think that would be so wonderful, Ian. We could talk about the dailies and you could be there on set to see me work. I think it could be so much fun for us."

Tilting her head back, I kiss her and press my forehead to hers. "You've convinced me. I'll tell Sheila to let them know the film can only be made if it's shot in the city."

"Oh, don't do that! What if they say no because of the cost? I'd hate to see Silk not get made because of my silly ideas."

I kiss her again and shake my head. "Then it never becomes a film. I'm fine with that too. As long as I have you, nothing else matters, Kristina."

And that's the absolute of my life now. As long as I have her by my side, I don't care about anything else. They can take everything away— the writing, the fame, the money. None of it matters as much as she does.

For so long, I've lived a comfortable but empty life. The drugs and alcohol did nothing to feed my starving soul, but I kept them as my constant companions because I needed something to fill the hollowness inside. That they never succeeded didn't matter. I could lie to myself and say everything was fine. I had money and fame. What else did I need?

But deep down I knew they weren't enough.

Then I saw Kristina that night and through a drunken haze I knew I had to have her. It wasn't love at first, but lust was better than what I'd been using to forget the emptiness. But it didn't take long for my feelings to grow far deeper until I couldn't be happy without her.

She stares up at me with a pensive look. "Ian, what's going to happen to us? Are we ever going to just be okay?"

I kiss her on the forehead and shake my head. "No. We're not the kind of people to just be okay."

Kristina knits her brows and sighs. "We can't keep going on like we have. Since the first night we met, we've been on some crazy emotional rollercoaster. Do you want to stay like that?"

"We can't help what we are. Something about the two of us together is crazy. But is that so bad?"

"I don't know. How long can crazy last? At some point, don't you want life to be like other people's?"

Shaking my head, I can't help but smile. A Hollywood star and an author would never be like other people. "Kristina, we aren't like other people. You're famous and I'm a recovering addict. I'll always be a recovering addict. We are who we are. That doesn't mean we can't be happy."

"But we've spent so much time unhappy. Don't you worry about that?"

I see the concern in her beautiful blue eyes.

"No. Love isn't about being happy all the time. Love is about getting through the bad times and appreciating the good times."

"We've been through so much bad, Ian. I just worry all of this is going to burn out one day soon. Don't you worry about that?"

"No, I don't because when all the bad is stripped away, we love each other madly with the kind of passion people only dream about. Most people never feel—I mean really feel anything. They say they love, but what they really do is stay in relationships that are boring but safe. That's not us. There's nothing safe about us."

"I want to think that we're always going to be okay, but I worry, Ian. What if someday one of us wants safe?"

"Do you want safe, Kristina?"

She remains silent for a long moment, closing her eyes as her mouth turns down into a frown. I run the pad of my thumb over the swell of her bottom lip while I wait to hear her answer knowing I can't promise her safe. That's the last thing I can offer her.

"I don't know if I want safe. I just worry about what happens down the road with us."

Leaning over, I press my lips to hers in a kiss full of how much I love her. "Nothing about us has ever been safe. What we feel is raw and rough and sometimes we break each other. I don't know what's going to happen down the road. I just know I don't want to think about my life without you in it, Kristina."

"I don't want to think of my life without you in it, Ian. I don't want safety if it means you and I aren't together. I just worry that someday one of us will break us and we won't know how to put the pieces back together."

I caress her cheek, loving the feel of her soft skin. "Maybe we're just going to have to accept the fact that we belong together, broken or not. We crash, we burn, and we break everything around us, but each time we search for one another because each of us has what the other needs."

Her eyes fill with a look of confusion. "What do I have that you need? I keep messing things up for us. How could you need that?"

"I need the sweetness that's so much a part of you. I need the strength you show when things get rough between us."

She rolls her eyes and scrunches up her nose. "What strength? I wish I was strong."

"Only a strong woman would have driven all this way in a blizzard to see someone she wasn't sure would even talk to her. You are strong, Kristina, and that strength is something I want in my life. I need it. I need you. If anyone should want to leave, it's you after what I put you through."

"No, I never wanted to leave. I know I said I would when you told me the truth about your addiction that night, but how could I leave when the man I love needed me most?"

Pulling her into my arms, I hold her to me and whisper, "You deserve so much better than what I've given you, but if you'll have me, I promise that's all in the past. I know you have no good reason to believe someone who freely admits he's always going to be a recovering heroin addict, but I mean every word."

She hugs me tightly to her and I feel her sob against my chest. "Oh Ian, how could I not want you? For all your weaknesses, you're the one person in this world who makes me feel like I'm something special."

I tilt her head back and look down into her beautiful face and smile for the simple reason that she makes me happy. "You are special. I knew that from the moment I first saw you on my television in that film. No matter who else was in the scene, you shined like no one else I'd ever seen before. I had to meet you."

"I thought it was because you wanted to sleep with me," she says with a chuckle as a blush covers the apples of her cheeks.

"There was that," I admit. "But I saw something else that night too, something that attracted me to you in a way that I'd never felt before with anyone."

"What was it?"

I think back to that night as I sat alone in my apartment like I did every other night and mindlessly stared at my TV until I saw her face. That moment is seared into my mind as the one when everything in my life changed. From then on, even when I became lost in the drugs again, I had someone who I never stopped thinking about. That had never been the case for me.

"Something in your eyes told me you might be able to accept who I was."

Kristina smiles and I see that gentleness in her eyes I saw that night. "I love that you saw something that no one else has ever seen in me, Ian."

"I'm glad all those other men missed that in you. If they didn't, you wouldn't be here with me right now."

"Did I ever tell you how nervous I was that night we met at that bar?"

I shake my head and chuckle. "No. I can't imagine why."

"When I heard you wanted to meet me, all I

could think about was that this incredibly talented author who'd written one of my favorite books would be sitting across the table from me and I'd feel like a total idiot in front of you. I was so worried you'd think I was just some stupid actress."

"There's nothing stupid about you. And you didn't have to worry. I was too busy being entirely sure you'd think I was just some boring history writer."

"I love the idea that we were both so unsure that night. Every man I've ever dated always seemed so sure of himself. So sure I would fall for him because he was good looking or famous. So sure he was too charming for me to say no to. But you were thinking of me when we met, just like I was thinking of you. That's the difference."

"Sounds pretty selfless for an addict and a movie star," I joke.

She looks down at the comforter and runs her fingers over the edge of the fabric. "I guess, but those are just labels for us, Ian. I like to think of the two of us as just people who care more than they should and finally found someone who really cares too."

"I've never been accused of caring too much. Never in my life has anyone thought that about me," I admit, suddenly ashamed of how truly selfish I am.

"I think you're very sensitive to other people. I know you don't show it a lot, but I've seen it since the moment we met. I saw it in your eyes when you looked at me that night in that booth." She lifts her hand to caress my cheek, smiling up at me now. "No one as passionate as you could ever be insensitive without trying. I like that I'm the only one who sees that side of you, though."

Her touch thrills me, as always, and I lean my head into her palm to feel more of her. I love that she sees me like that. I don't know if it's the truth, but if it isn't, it's the best lie I've ever been told.

"Now you see what I mean when I say that being with you lets me be the man I always wanted to be."

Kristina presses her lips to mine and whispers, "I love that man, Ian. I love how smart he is and how he understands me like no one else ever has. And even if we freeze to death here in this cabin in the middle of a blizzard, I want to say thank you for making me feel adored like no one else in the world."

Pulling her closer to keep her warm, I hold her to me so she can take some of my warmth. "We're not going to freeze here. There's no way we've been through all we've been through just to find happiness in time to freeze in a snowstorm.

The electricity will come on again, and then we'll eat the dinner you cooked and talk about what we want to do when we get back to the city."

Her body shivers against mine, and I silently wonder if any of that will actually happen. It's only been about an hour, but the heat from the fireplace is quickly becoming too little to keep us warm. It won't take long before a down comforter and a pile of blankets won't be enough.

As we sit there, I wonder if this will be the end of us. Not exactly the way I thought I'd go. I would have put a hefty bet on my dying alone in my apartment from an overdose of heroin. I figured they'd find me partially decomposed after weeks of lying dead on my living room floor, the stench of my rotting corpse too much for even that one gruff and seasoned EMT worker there always is on the scene. Everyone would wonder how someone like me could die alone without a soul in the world curious enough to come by for weeks as I lay sprawled out, finally dead from the drugs.

"Hey, you got quiet all of a sudden. What's wrong?"

I look down at Kristina resting her head on my shoulder and smile. "Nothing. Just trying to remember my Boy Scout days in case things get really bad with this storm."

She giggles in that way that never fails to charm me and says, "I love the idea of you being a little boy in his Boy Scout uniform out in the woods. So what did you remember that will help us if it gets colder in here?"

"Not much, except for a few knots, which I don't think will help us keep warm."

"Knots, huh?" she asks with a twinkle in her eye like she's heard something intriguing.

"Yeah, but that won't keep us warm."

"True, but when we get back to the city it might make for an interesting time."

I kiss her on the tip of her nose and grin, loving this side of her. "Does my Kristina like being tied up? And how did I not know this by now?"

A sheepish look comes over her face and she bites her bottom lip. "I don't know if I do since nobody's ever done that to me, but Sienna was telling me something a while back about this thing she and her boyfriend did that sounded interesting."

"So you have a kinky friend named Sienna? Sienna who?"

"Sienna Rollins. She's an actress like me."

I think back to the countless hours I've spent on Netflix and try to place the name, but it doesn't ring a bell. "I don't think I've ever heard of her."

Proudly, Kristina says, "You will. She's a knockout blond with everything going for her and on top of all that, she's a great actress. All she needs is the right part and she's going to be a household name."

"Like you."

"Sienna's so much better than I am. She just needs the break we all wait for and she's going to set the world on fire. I just know it."

"I think it's great you're so generous like that, Kristina. I can't imagine most actors and actresses are like you."

"Sienna's my friend. I want to see good things happen for her. That's how I am with people I care about."

The lights around us flicker on and off and then come back on, ending the threat of our freezing to death out in the wilds of upstate New York. Kristina looks around and breathes a sigh of relief.

"I was starting to worry for a while there. How about I get up and see if I can get that roast in shape so we can eat?"

As she moves to leave my side, I hold her there next to me, not for warmth but because I have something I need to say. "In a minute. I want to ask you something first."

Her eyes show her worry at what my question might be, but she presses a smile onto her lips. "Okay. Shoot."

"I don't want you to think I'm saying any of this because we almost froze here because I never believed that would happen. I'm saying this because if I don't ask now and somehow I mess things up, I'll regret it for the rest of my life."

"Okay. What do you want to ask me?"

Taking her hands in mine, I bring them to my lips and kiss them before taking a deep breath. "Kristina, will you come live with me? Be my muse forever. I want to see your face when I open my eyes each morning and feel you next to me as I go to sleep each night, and in between I want the chance to show you every day how much I love you."

Tears well in her eyes and she nods her head. "Yes, I will, Ian. I will be your muse forever."

As I take her in my arms, I feel happier than I've ever felt in my life. No drug has ever made me feel like this. Only knowing Kristina loves me like I love her could make me feel so incredible.

"I love you, Ian," she whispers in my ear while I hold her tightly to me. "For all the good and all the bad we've been through, I love you with all my heart."

"I love you too, my beautiful muse. My Kristina."

CHAPTER SEVEN

Kristina

THE ROAST SOMEHOW made it through the electricity going out and as we sit down to eat, I see Ian's eyes open wide at the sight of the meal I've prepared. Looking at me, he asks, "Is it possible you're the perfect woman? Gorgeous, talented, sexy, and a great cook?"

I sit down across from him at the kitchen table and smile at his comment. "I thought the same thing that first night you made me your world famous risotto."

"That sounded pretty sexist, didn't it? I didn't mean it like that. I think anyone with all those qualities, man or woman, is pretty damn impressive."

Waving away his worry that he offended me, I say, "Not to worry. Eat up. We never know how long the electricity is going to stay on since it's still blowing around out there, and I'd hate for this meal to go to waste."

"I have an idea. Hang on," he says as he jumps out of his chair to head for a closet in the hallway. He returns a few seconds later with two white taper candles and two silver candlesticks. Placing them between us in the middle of the table, he walks to the fireplace and brings over one long matchstick. As he lights the two candles, he says sweetly, "This wonderful meal calls for candlelight, so even if the electricity goes out, we'll still have a romantic dinner for two."

When he shows this side of him—the cute and thoughtful side—I can't help falling in love with him all over again. I know his demons will never really disappear, always hiding deep inside and looking for that perfect opportunity to come out and wreak havoc on him again, but I love him. The good, the bad, and the worst of him. I love all of it.

"I love it, Ian. It's perfect."

By the time we finish our dinner, he's convinced I am the perfect woman, and even though I know I'm nowhere close to being that, I'm happy to let him think that. He sits across from me with a completely satisfied look in his eyes, and I like that I could make that happen.

"Would you like to hear what I'm going to write for the second Silk book?" he asks as I clear the plates from the table.

"You know what the story is now?"

"I think so. Would you like to hear about it?"

I quickly run some hot water over the dirty dishes and return to my seat to hear all about his new book. "Yes! I'm dying to know what happens to Kate and Sean. You didn't give them a happily ever after in the first book, so will they get one in this book?"

Ian nods as a sexy grin spreads across his lips. "Yes. They'll get their happily ever after in this one. Not that I'm going to make it easy for them. They're going to have to get through a lot of obstacles before they find their happiness."

"Sort of like us?"

"Exactly like us. It is our story, after all."

A feeling of dread comes over me for a moment. "Does that mean you're going to have her go back to her addiction?"

The smile he wore just a few seconds earlier fades and he knits his brows. "Yeah. Kate's going to have to get through her heroin addiction to find real happiness with Sean."

I instantly begin to worry that writing about that will be too much for Ian. Will he want to go back to it himself because he's living it again through his character? Will he give in to the temptation?

He reaches across the table and clutches my

hand. "Don't worry. I'll be okay. You'll be right there with me, and every day I'll read you what I wrote. I think it will be good for me."

"How?"

"This part of me is never going away, Kristina. I need to be able to live with the reality of who I can be and what it will do to my life if I let myself go back to that. Don't worry. I know what I can lose if I do."

"You mean me?"

"I know you stayed last time, but I'm not a fool. I know how bad that was for you, and there's no reason for me to believe you'll stay if it happens again, no matter how much you love me. I won't risk that again. I promise."

"I'm just worried it will bring back all those feelings and be too much for you."

Ian takes a deep breath and slowly exhales as concern settles into his expression. "I know. And it might bring back a lot of things I wish I could forget, but my desire for that poison isn't something I can just pretend never existed. It did, and it will for the rest of my life. That's how addiction is."

I hate hearing him say he'll always want that awful drug. Of all the things about his addiction, that's the worst. Knowing no matter how much he fights it and how long he stays clean, somewhere inside him is a part that will always want it.

He comes around the table and kneeling next to me, looks up at me with those dark eyes that always seem so full of passion. "I promise, Kristina. No more of that. I'll do whatever I have to do to fight those demons. I choose you—I choose us—over that shit. I don't want to lose you and all the wonderful things being with you makes me feel."

Cradling his face, I can't help but believe him. He's the man I love. I just pray to God he's telling the truth.

"I want more than anything for you to never touch that stuff again, Ian. You're such a wonderful man. You're a good person, and I think you believe what you say. I want you to be happy, and I've never seen you so miserable as when you were high. That man wasn't the Ian I know. That man was so lost, and I didn't know how to get to him."

He covers my hands with his and nods his understanding. "I know. I don't want that for us. I want us to be happy, and I know heroin has no place in any happiness we'll ever have. I just want you to know I haven't done anything this time. We ran into a problem and I came here, but I didn't go back to it."

I quietly admit what had been in the back of my mind since hearing he left the city. "I was afraid you might have. More than the snowstorm and even the chance that you might turn me away, I feared I'd find you high and lost to me again."

"I didn't do it. I swear. I'm not going to tell you I didn't try to get blasted drunk to forget how hurt I was, but nothing else. I promise. Never again."

Leaning down, I kiss him and say, "I'm so sorry for what happened. I never meant to hurt you. I love you."

His smile tells me he's truly forgiven me. "I know I'm as much to blame. You deserved more than a junkie."

"Promise me something?"

"Anything."

"Promise me we can forget all this and be happy again. I want us to be happy like we used to be before everything got all messed up."

"I promise. This is a new chance for us. We're starting over and have the ability to be as happy as we want."

"Good. You know what I want now?"

He understands the tone in my voice and slowly runs his hands up over my thighs. "I think I know, but why don't you tell me what you want?"

A tiny moan escapes my throat as his thumbs graze the very tops of my legs. "I want my gorgeous author boyfriend to make love to me over there on that couch in front of the fire."

"Your wish is my command, my muse." Ian stands and holds his hand out for me to take it. I weave my fingers through his, and he asks, "Anything in particular you'd like?"

As he guides me to the couch, I think about his question and there isn't anything in particular I want. Other than him completely lost in me and me completely lost in him.

He turns to face me and kisses me deeply, nearly taking my breath away and making my knees go weak. "I'm going to worship every beautiful inch of your body. When I'm done with you, you won't be able to think of anything but how much I love you. Now lie back and let me get down to work."

I do as he commands and lie back on the couch. Crawling up my body, he gently pulls my sweater over my head, leaving me naked in front of him.

Beginning at my ankles, he slowly kisses up one leg and then the other until his mouth is ever so close to my excited pussy. I let my legs fall open to the sides, eager for him to press his mouth to my clit and give me what I want, but he has other plans.

He looks up at me as he nips at the tender skin of my left thigh and then says, "I know I told you this before, but your cunt is the prettiest pink I've ever seen in my life. Just seeing it makes me want to bury my face in you."

"I wish you would."

"Not yet. I want your body primed for me, so sit back and let yourself enjoy what I'm about to do."

I watch as he drags his tongue up toward my core, stopping just as his mouth reaches the crease of my leg. Over and over, he teases me like this, every so often letting his lips graze my pussy lightly and making me want him so fucking badly. No matter how much I whimper and beg, he still persists in teasing me, but I know the waiting will be worth it.

When he finally presses his mouth to me, it's like heaven. His tongue flat, he drags it up over my tender skin, moaning against my body until he reaches my clit. I watch in rapt attention as he hovers over that point of perfect pleasure and gazes up at me with a look of the devil in his eyes.

"Ready or should I wait a little more?"

I bury my hands in his hair and pull his head toward my body, dying to feel his mouth on me.

He doesn't resist at all, as hungry for me as I am for him, and the first touch of his tongue on my clit sends a jolt of pleasure racing through my body like electricity coursing through me.

My fingertips tingle as he sucks my clit between his lips, and just as I'm sure I can't take another second of this sweet torture, he gently bites down and it's like fireworks exploding behind my eyes as my orgasm takes me over. I ride his mouth as waves of pleasure wash over me, and as the exquisite tremors begin to subside, he flicks his tongue and slides two fingers inside me, curling them perfectly against that sweet spot he knows will make me come again.

And then I come for the second time, this time even harder than the first, my hands holding his head so I don't miss a moment of the pleasure his mouth provides. Time ceases to exist in those moments when I feel like I'm floating above myself, and when he finally sits back away from me, I can't imagine how I'm going to continue feeling like this.

I open my eyes to see him smacking his lips like he's just enjoyed a favorite treat. He grins like a naughty schoolboy, and I can't help but smile.

"You look like the cat who just ate the canary," I tease.

"I love the taste of you on my tongue." He

brings his fingers to his mouth and sucks me off them. "I want you to know that just in case I someday have some kind of difficulty getting it up that I'll be more than happy to spend all my time making you come that way."

Reaching out for him, I take him by the hand to pull him down on top of me. "I do love that, but I think I'd miss the feeling of you inside me. We'll just have to get you the little blue pill."

His hard cock nudges up against me, and Ian groans in my ear, "Thankfully, that's not a problem I have now. Now my cock gets hard every time you're anywhere nearby."

I spread my legs wide to take him inside me, and he lifts his hips off the couch. I want to feel him fill me like only he can, but in my ear I hear him say, "I want you on my lap like the first time we were together."

Sitting up, he pulls me on top of him and in a second my thighs are straddling him as his cock waits for me so sit down on him. Slowly, I lower myself down and feel him enter me, filling me until there's no space between us and we're together in the most intimate way.

I kiss him and taste myself on his lips and tongue as he begins to thrust his cock in and out of me. His hands hold my hips firmly, and in my ear he moans, "I love it when you ride me like this. Let me watch you come apart for me, Kristina."

Raising myself up, I slide down his cock again as he sucks a nipple hard into his mouth. He knows what I like and what gets me off, and he gives it to me like no one else ever has. I ride him, my hips rocking back and forth, while he bites down on my excited nipple, sending waves of delight rushing through my body.

I watch him move from one breast to the other, each one receiving his attention and ratcheting up my desire with every gentle nip of my skin. The mouth that just brought me such pleasure now gives me the pain I crave to get off.

Inside, my orgasm begins to unwind slowly like coiled snake until I'm bucking wildly on his lap needing the release I know he can give me. Leaning back, he watches me inch toward that moment of sweet abandon, all the while guiding my movement with his hands on my hips. I'm so close. Just a few more passes of his cock over that spot inside me and I'll come apart.

Ian lets go of my left hip and moves his hand between us. Sliding his finger over my swollen and needy clit, his touch finally sends me over the edge and my orgasm explodes inside me. I throw my head back as every nerve in my body comes alive and focuses on that spot where his fingertip still rests.

For a long moment, I forget everything but him inside me. I forget all the good and the bad we've been through. I forget the drugs and Cilla's betrayal. I forget everything that tore us apart and all I can think of is how incredible my body feels on his.

"I love watching you when you come. You're so erotic and sensual, just like a woman should be."

I open my eyes and look down at me staring up at me with wonder in his eyes, like what I am to him is something amazing. Leaning down, I kiss him and say, "Only with you. I've never been like this with anyone else. I think it's you who makes me feel that way."

"What way?"

"Sensual. Like I'm sexy and it's something that feels natural."

"Good because it is something natural. I see it every time we're together, and I love it. I love that you never pretend to be something other than what you are."

I look down at where his body and mine are still joined and frown. "You didn't come."

"I had to work at it, if that makes you feel better about my not coming. I almost couldn't hold back at one point."

"Why did you then?" I say, pouting because I love when I can make him come that way.

"Because as much as I enjoy coming from being inside you, I love coming from your mouth even more. You know that."

"I think you have an unhealthy obsession with my going down on you, Ian."

"I think you love it as much as I do."

What I love is that when I suck his cock he's happy. I still wonder from time to time if I'm really any good at it or if he's just inclined to come easier that way, but it doesn't matter. No man has ever taken my body to the heights he has, so if my going down on him gives him pleasure, who am I to say it shouldn't be that way?

I lift myself off him and look down to see his cock glistening with my juices. Lowering myself to the floor, I wrap my fingers around him and look up to see him watching me as if he can't wait for me to put my mouth on his skin. For so long I thought this part of sex demeaning to women, an act that made us subservient and less than the man, but now I see with the right person, it's just another way to bring the man you adore pleasure.

And as I watch him come, I know this is something even he doesn't realize means something to me. That my touch, my mouth, can excite him and I can take all he has makes me feel like that sensual being I've always wanted to be.

CHAPTER EIGHT

Ian

WE LIE IN each other's arms after a third night straight of lovemaking that only reinforced how much I love Kristina. No other woman has ever made me feel so entirely devoted to her happiness, and although it's not my usual way of feeling, I genuinely enjoy being the reason she smiles.

Me. Ian Anwell. The reason someone so incredibly sweet and gentle is happy. As I feel her move against me and make that adorable snoring noise, I have a hard time believing I could be so lucky.

The storm outside ended two days ago, so the roads should be passable enough to let us leave and start our life together back in my apartment. I've had enough of the sticks.

I gently smooth my hand over her soft hair, caressing her back up and down and feeling more content than I could ever imagine being. Today, we'll drive back to the city and move her into my apartment, and after a few days of settling in, which I intend on spending in bed as much as possible, I'll get working on Silk and Steel in earnest and see what magic Sheila can work with Silk.

For the first time in my adult life, I can't wait for what's about to happen.

Kristina stirs and gazes up at me with a questioning look in her blue eyes. "I woke you up, didn't I?"

"No, not this time. I've been awake for a while."

She blushes in her adorable way and smiles. "Good. I thought my snoring woke you up again. Are you sure you want me to move in knowing I spend my nights as a little chainsaw?"

Pulling her to me, I press a kiss to the top of her head. "I'm sure I can't wait to have you live with me. I was just thinking about it, in fact."

"I can't wait either, Ian."

I slide under her and my hands travel down her back to squeeze her ass. "Me too. I'll cook every night for you after I write all day, and we'll spend long hours making love in every room and on every surface. And in the mornings, we'll get up and fuck like crazy people in that shower you love."

Biting her lip, she smiles at my plans and asks, "What about when I have to work?"

"Then I'll text you too many times a day and tell you how much I love you, and when you come home, I'll cook for you and we'll make love over and over every night to make up for all the time you were away. And I'll tell you every morning how much I love waking up next to you."

"Your little chainsaw," she says with a giggle.

I kiss her softly and nuzzle her neck. "My little chainsaw."

This is what we can be when the madness we are subsides for even a short time. Sweetness and love. I could spend the rest of my life just like this with her cuddled up against me.

"What about when we fight?"

I take a deep breath in. "We'll never fight."

Kristina looks at me and shakes her head, her expression serious now. "You know we're going to fight, Ian. What's going to happen when we do?"

"We'll fight like we love. Completely. Madly. Wildly. And if the fight is my fault, I promise to only be an asshole for twenty-four hours. But you need to remember who I am, Kristina. I'm going to be jealous of other men I think want you. I'm going to be possessive when I shouldn't be, even though I won't want to be. You're my addiction."

She kisses me and cups my face with her hands. "And I promise to love you even when we're fighting completely, madly, and wildly because you're the only man I want to be with."

We stay there silent in each other's arms with the knowledge that no matter what happens, who we are will always be based on the love we have for one another. It's raw and ragged sometimes, and smooth as silk at other times, but it's always the most honest emotion we share between us.

I love her with utterly all I have, and she loves me with all she has. Anything less for us wouldn't be real.

Breaking the silence, I whisper in her ear, "Although I'd usually say we should stay here and enjoy ourselves, I think we should get back to the city as soon as we can. The storm's over, so I think we can leave whenever we're ready."

She rolls off me and kisses my cheek. "Okay. Give me a little bit and I'll be ready to go. I just have to grab a shower and get back into my clothes. They should be dry by now."

"You don't want me to go out to the car and get your bag?"

"No, it's okay. As long as I don't have to put on wet clothes, I'll be fine."

I love it when she's cute, and as she slips from the bed, she flashes me an adorable smile. "It's not like I've spent much time in them since I got here."

An hour later after I've dug both vehicles out of the snow drifts that nearly cover my car, we're ready to go back to reality, which includes the media mess we ran away from just a few days ago. I check the fireplace and turn off the lights, already missing our time here, but no matter what we have to deal with back in the city, we have each other.

And that's all that matters.

Kristina stands at the front door waiting for me, and wrapping my arms around her, I pull her close. "Ready?"

She looks up into my eyes with worry written all over her face. "Do you think we should stay longer to let all that business die down back there?"

"No. I am who I am, and that's not going to change. As Ian Anwell, I write historical fiction, and as T. Anderson, I wrote our story and I'm writing even more of it. It is what it is. As long as I know you're by my side, everything will be fine. So let's go back and show the world we're together and then hope they go away."

"What if they don't?"

"Then that gives us even more reasons to stay inside in bed. I wouldn't worry, though. Today we might be newsworthy, but trust me. There will be a celebrity who does something tomorrow that will make us as boring as yesterday's news. That you can depend on."

"Okay. I'll follow you and after I give Sienna her car back, I'll just go to your place. I have a suitcase full of clothes and everything I need, so I'm all set. I can go to my apartment in a few days."

"Perfect. Be careful on the hill. I've driven that road in the snow a few times and it can be treacherous."

With a big smile, she says, "Got it! I'm more worried about you, though. Sienna's SUV is made for this type of weather, but all you have is a car."

"Don't worry about me. I grew up around this type of weather, so I know how to handle it. Ready?"

She kisses me sweetly and buttons up the last button on her coat. "Ready. See you in a few."

THE ROADS LEADING back to the city aren't as bad as I'd feared they'd be, and as I drive I can't help but daydream about how life has turned out. What began as my obsession with Kristina as she acted on my television screen has become the kind of love I never believed someone like me would ever have. Addicts just don't get those happily ever afters. Not in real life, anyway. Only in books and in movies do they get that second chance because of a great woman who truly loves them. The reality is usually far harsher.

A life alone always fighting the demons that live inside and want more than anything to resurface and take over.

But that's not me anymore. Yes, I'll always be a recovering heroin addict. That's a truth that will never go away, so I have no choice. I have to face it. But I'm more than that, and for a long time I didn't think I was.

Until Kristina. She makes me see no matter what that junk offers, I can have better. I want better. I want that elusive happily ever after so popular in the fiction I write and the movies she makes and so rare in real life.

I look in the rearview mirror to see her behind me smiling like she knows I'm looking back at her. I wave and watch her wave back and blow me a kiss. Even such a small gesture makes my heart swell with the happiness only she can give me.

But then her expression morphs into one of horror, and in a flash, everything changes. Like some slow-motion replay, I take my gaze from her back to the road and see the truck rounding the turn into our lane. I swerve to avoid it, but it's no use. He's going too fast and he sideswipes the car, tearing off the mirror next to me. His front end rips down the side of my car, and the noise of metal crushing metal fills my ears.

I lose control and then there's only spinning. Frantically, I try to see Kristina, but it's all happening so fast now. At some point, I don't hear the screeching sound of metal on metal anymore, and everything becomes a blur. I press on the brake over and over, but it's no use. I crash through the guardrail and careen down the side of an embankment.

Trees fly by me as visions of my life rush through my mind. They're just pieces of my life, actually, but they make up the whole of who I am.

Me with my parents at the house I grew up in on a spring day, the sun warming my face as my father tossed a baseball toward my glove.

The day I graduated with honors from Cornell and the look of sadness on my mother's face when she congratulated me, wishing my father could have lived long enough to see that day too.

Standing in the rain at my father's grave later that day with my diploma and hoping somehow he saw what I'd achieved.

The moment I learned my first book would be published.

That first time I tried heroin and the euphoric sensation of flying it brought with it.

The feeling of complete and utter failure as I walked into rehab the last time.

Alone in my apartment and seeing the most beautiful woman in the world appear on my television screen for the first time.

My mind's a jumble of fear and confusion, but somewhere in all that fleeting memories of my time with Kristina begin to appear in my mind. They calm me so as my car finally hits the bottom of the ravine and the air bag explodes into me, I'm relaxed. As the shock of what happened settles into me, I feel my head fall forward toward the inflated air bag and then there's nothing but darkness.

Kristina sits next to me quietly reading what I wrote that afternoon as I absentmindedly play with the ends of her hair, twirling them around my finger and then releasing them to do it again. I'm nervous to hear her thoughts and opinions on the story so far. Will she like it or will she think it's useless drivel that makes her question agreeing to be my muse?

I call Silk our story, but in truth it's hers. I write only because she inspires me. Without her, there is no Silk. Without her, there is no story to be told.

If she knew how much she means to me. I say the words I love you, but they never seem to be enough to convey what I feel for her. They're hackneyed and tired, overused by people who have no idea what love is and desperate souls who think they're some kind of magic to keep others in their lives long after they've decided they no longer want to stick around.

I wish I knew better words for how she makes me feel. Yes, I love her, but it's more than just that. I love her. I adore her. She brings out the best in me, things I never knew existed inside me or were possible for me. I'm the man I've always dreamed of being with her.

Because of her.

Turning to face me, she looks at me with watery eyes. Is she sad? Does the story I've written about her make her unhappy?

"Ian, this is beautiful," she says in a quiet voice, instantly calming my fears. "I love this story. You've made Kate everything I wish I ever was. She's strong and fearless, but she loves Sean with everything she has."

"Do you like Sean? Do you think I wrote him the right way for her? I want the reader to see how much he goes through for her and still loves her more than even he can understand."

Kristina's smile lights up her face. "Oh yes! He's just what she needs. The part where she won't let him in because she's afraid that her feelings aren't what his are made me cry. She kept telling him that he didn't want her and that she was no good for him, but he knew the truth. He knew she didn't just care about the physical thing between them. He knew there was more. I love that."

I kiss her gently on the lips and take a deep breath in, happy my muse loves the story I've written because of her.

"What happens next? Do you know?" she asks as she leans her head on my shoulder. "I want to hear all about it."

I lean my head on hers and close my laptop. "Not yet. The story isn't finished. I have some more to write."

"Will they end up happy, Ian? Is that how this ends?"

"I don't know yet. I haven't written the rest of their story."

Kristina wraps her arms around my waist and sighs. "I want them to be happy."

I open my eyes, unsure of where I am. Sharp pain tears through the top of my head. I run my palm over my cheek and pull my hand away to see blood. Slowly, the accident filters through my brain and I remember being run off the road and sent down the embankment. I look around to see if anyone has come to help and see the back of Kristina's SUV nearby on fire.

PANIC RUSHES THROUGH me at the thought that

she's trapped in there. I need to get out of this fucking car to help her! I try to move, but my left arm is stuck between the door and the seat. It should hurt, I think, but that doesn't matter now. I have to get to Kristina.

I pound on the window hoping someone will hear me. I can't watch her burn to death in that car and not do anything, so I scream, "Help! Help us! Get her out of there!"

My voice begins to give out I scream so loud, but a terrifying thought creeps into my mind as I see the flames engulf Kristina's car. Help won't arrive in time to save her and I can't save her trapped here. She'll die because I couldn't save her.

Why isn't she screaming for help? Tears come to my eyes as the thought of her already dead from the accident forms in my brain. No. God, no! Don't let her be dead already.

"Kristina! Can you hear me? Answer me! Kristina!" I yell as loud as I can and hope she hears my pleas. But I hear nothing in return.

I begin to feel weak and keeping my eyes open becomes difficult. Somewhere nearby the sound of sirens floats down to where we wait, but it's too late.

My eyes close as I accept the reality. It's too late.

CHAPTER NINE

Ian

I OPEN MY eyes slowly to see the stark white walls surrounding me. I don't know this place or where I am. I'm in a bed, and I hear machines beeping and buzzing around my head. Directly in front of me is a window but not to the outside.

I'm in a hospital.

"Ian, can you hear me?" a gentle voice asks.

I turn to see an older woman leaning over me with a look of happiness on her face, which I hope means whatever I'm in the hospital for isn't going to kill me. Her soft brown eyes stare down into mine as she waits for my answer, and I nod.

"Yes," I croak out, my throat instantly hurting from just that one word.

As I raise my hand to massage my throat, the woman moves over to a table and quickly returns with a cup of water. "Here, drink this. Your throat is tight because you haven't spoken for a while."

I take a sip of water and close my eyes as it slowly hydrates my parched throat. A few more sips and I feel ready to risk speaking again. Swallowing hard, I say, "Where am I?"

"Columbia Memorial. You've been here for nearly five days."

Five days? But I don't recognize the hospital name as one in the city. "Where is this hospital?"

"Hudson, New York."

My mind races through memories of that day when my car careened off the side of that mountain road. I look down in horror at my left arm and remember it mangled and bloody. Now all I see are bandages.

Confused, I ask her, "My arm?"

The look of happiness on the woman's face morphs into one of concern, and she presses a fake smile onto her worried face. "They tried...I think I better let the doctor answer your questions. Let me go find him."

As she moves away toward the door, I reach out with my right hand to grab her arm and say, "I need to find out about Kristina. Is she okay? What happened to her?"

"I'm sorry. Let me get the doctor and he can help you. Just one minute."

She hurries from the room with an expression that tells me she's as confused as I am, but why? Is it because they couldn't save her?

I lay there for over an hour waiting for someone to come in and explain what's going on, all the while my heart sinking lower and lower at the thought that Kristina's gone. She's gone because I couldn't save her.

I see Sheila stop in front of the window to my room. When our eyes meet, she begins to cry and covers her face, which makes me sure however I may feel that I don't look as good as I think I do.

She walks into the room slowly, wiping her tears from her cheeks as she approaches the side of my bed. Dressed in jeans and a short sleeve blue and white print top, she looks like she always has. Not incredibly feminine or even attractive, but like herself.

"Oh, Ian! What happened? How do you feel? Do you know who I am?" she says on a sob as she squeezes my hand.

"Of course. You're my agent, Sheila Rogers."

"Yes, yes! They didn't know if you'd have any permanent brain damage after the accident. It was awful! I got the call that you'd crashed your car down a ravine and I rushed up here. I've hoped every day that you'd finally wake up."

"Where's Kristina? I need to see her. Is she here? Did they bring her here?"

Sheila gives me the same confused look that

the other woman did and says nothing for a few moments. When she finally speaks, her words make no sense.

"I don't know, Ian. Was she in the car with you?"

"No, she was following me and that truck must have run her off the road too. Her car was on fire. Did they get to her in time? Where is she?"

After a few more moments of silence, Sheila quietly says, "I don't know, Ian. I just knew you were in the accident."

"I need to speak to her. I need to know she's okay," I say as I begin to feel real fear that she's not safe.

"Okay, okay. Don't get yourself upset. You just woke up. Take your time."

"I don't want to take my time! I need to see her. I need to let her know I'm okay and see she's okay."

Sheila closes the door and returns to my bedside. Pulling up a chair, she sits down next to me and sighs. "Ian, I'll see what I can find out. What do you remember?"

I try to remember the details of the accident, but my brain seems fuzzy on the details, so I just tell her what I know. "I was in a car accident coming back from the cabin after you told me to get out of the city. Not that I'm blaming you, but you seem a little confused about what happened. The car slid off the road and down the embankment. Kristina was following me in her car and I saw it on fire."

Sheila gives my hand a sympathetic squeeze and frowns. "Honey, I'll see what I can find out. I just know I got a call saying you'd been in an accident. There was no mention of anyone else."

I shake my head, refusing to believe what she's saying. "No. She was in the car behind me, Sheila. I need to know what happened to her."

Sheila takes my hand to calm me down, but I can't stay in that bed. I need to find Kristina and know she's okay. I don't care that I've got tubes and wires all over me. Slowly, I move my legs to try to get out of bed, but she stops me.

"Ian, please. I need you to relax. I'll help you find out what happened, but I need you to stay in bed until the doctor comes in."

"Please find out. I need to know she's okay. Why won't anyone tell me what happened to her?"

"Okay, I'll help you. I promise."

My chest feels like someone's hit me with a sledgehammer. I struggle to catch my breath as the thought that Kristina is gone fills my mind and I mumble, "I think I'm feeling tired now. I'm just going to close my eyes for a little bit. Do me a favor and tell the doctors to let me sleep, okay? They can do their tests and ask their questions later."

She nods and gives me her best fake but sympathetic smile. "Okay, Ian. I'll tell them."

I roll over and close my eyes to block out everything. Who I am. What my life is now if Kristina isn't in it. How little I have to go back to.

That the woman I love may not even be alive anymore.

TWO UNSUCCESSFUL SURGERIES to fix the nerve damage in my left arm and three months of physical therapy to learn how to live without the use of it and now for the first time in what seems like forever, I'm back at my apartment. Unlike everything else in my world since I woke up in that hospital bed, it's the same as I remember. At least there's that. I might have gone into shock if I opened the door and saw LL Bean décor all over the fucking place.

The evidence of Sheila's handiwork in keeping my apartment clean after my accident can be seen in every spotless nook and cranny of my home. I've spent enough nights face down on the floor to know it never looked this clean. I feel like I've walked into some kind of showroom apartment realtors use to hook prospective buyers.

In some way, I'm a stranger in my own home it's been so long since I've been here. I look around and see Kristina everywhere. Sheila hasn't been able to find out what happened to her, so I don't even know if she's still alive. Since the accident, she's never called or come to visit or even sent a message through Sheila.

All I have of her are memories. In my love for her, I literally am alone, but now that I'm home, I plan on finding out what happened. As I have every day since I woke up in that hospital bed, I try her number but all it does is ring without anyone answering.

After walking around my place studying it like some kind of tourist in a museum, I feel drawn to the living room and sit down on the couch. I have no idea if this is what I should do. Maybe I should write. Maybe I should sleep more.

All I know is I'm alone and can do anything or nothing. My life is a blank slate.

I should consider myself lucky. How many people would kill to have enough money to do whatever they desire in life and a marketable skill if they choose to use it? How many would love to begin life anew with the chance to start all over again?

Neither of these ideas give me any comfort, though. I don't think of myself as lucky. I think of myself as someone who had everything he ever wanted and through some terrible twist of fate had it all taken away from him. I had love and happiness, and now I have neither.

I close my eyes and lean my head against the back of the couch as I try to stay sane. Sheila's biggest fear is that I'll turn back to heroin again, but I don't want that now. I don't even really want a drink now. All I want is a way to find what I've lost before I completely lose my fucking mind.

Grabbing the TV remote from the coffee table in front of me, I turn it on and immediately the Netflix screen appears and tells the story of what I'd been doing the last time I sat there in front of that screen. All of Kristina's films are there, watched but ready for me to see them again.

I choose the remake of The Misfits and sit back to wait for her to appear in front of me. My palms begins to sweat and my heart slams against my chest as each minute ticks by, and then there she is in front of me again, those beautiful cornflower blue eyes looking out as if she sees me watching her.

When she smiles, my heart fills with joy at the memory of the two of us alone and her smiling like that for me. But where is she now? I need to find her. She belongs in my arms, smiling up at me as I hold her. I need to see her look at me with those soft blue eyes and tell me she loves me.

I believe she's still alive. She has to be.

I can find nothing online that says anything about what happened to her. No mention of her death. No mention of any accident at all. Did I just imagine it all in a state of shock as I sat there at the bottom of that embankment after the accident? But if that's the case, why didn't she come to see me even once while I was in the hospital all those weeks and then the three months of rehab for my arm?

I call Albert and get him moving on the only thing that matters to me. Finding Kristina. "Albert, I need you to contact Kristina Richards's agent, publicist, manager and anyone else who might know where she is. I have to find out."

"Okay, Ian. I can do that. You feeling okay?"

Albert's newfound interest in how I feel seems genuine, but I don't want to discuss my physical or mental well-being with him now. "Yeah, I'm fine. I just need you to find out where she is."

"Okay. Give me some time and I'll see what I can find out."

I pull my laptop out sometime after the first twenty-four hour Kristina Richards film marathon and attempt to type. The nerve damage in my left hand makes it impossible. The fingers on that hand just sit on the keyboard, useless now. I have all these ideas for the Silk and Steel story ready to pour out through my fingers, but with only working hand, I can barely write a page in two hours. Desperate to get the words out of my head, I find a pen and paper and write like I've never written before in my life. My mind works at a fevered pace, so at least I can say something good came from all of this misery.

Afterward, I'm exhausted and for two days, I sit and stare at the TV as I watch every film of hers and periodically answer Sheila's phone calls meant to calm her fears and ensure I'm not doing anything terrible to myself. But it's Albert's phone call I wait for.

"Ian, how are you feeling? Are you getting back to writing yet?" Sheila asks in that angelic voice of hers that makes the three times daily calls to check up on me not so bad.

"Maybe, but don't worry. I'm not doing anything illegal or harmful to myself," I say with a chuckle, doing my best to make her feel better about her task.

"Is there anything you need?"

I hesitate for a moment, but then answer, "No, I'm fine, Sheila." I'm anything but fine, but as soon as I hear from Albert, I'll be better.

At least I hope so.

The phone is silent for a long moment, and then she says, "I'm worried about you, Ian. I've never heard you sound so sad."

"I'm not back to the heroin, Sheila. I swear."

Sheila stays silent again and then says, "I'm so happy to hear that, Ian. Don't worry. Everything's going to be okay for you. You have a second chance, and now that you're back home, I'm going to be working overtime to make sure I get you the deal you deserve for Silk and get that film made, if possible."

Her mention of Silk makes my breath catch in my chest. The story of my love for Kristina. Our story.

I continue watching Kristina's films and wonder if I'm slowly losing my mind. All of this seems so familiar, yet it's been months. Thank God for Netflix, my old friend. It's the only way I can keep her in my life for now until Albert finds out where she is.

My phone rings, startling me out of my thoughts of just how miserable I truly am, and I see it's Albert calling back.

"Ian, I talked to all her people. They won't tell me where she is, but I have a friend I asked about her and he says he's heard she's left the city to live upstate."

"Really? Where?" I want to ask with who, but I can't bring myself to say the words.

"I don't know yet, but I asked him to find out. I'll let you know the minute I find out."

I return to my miserable existence, a sad loop of watching her films and then writing the continuation of our story. The words come slower now as I sink into what very well might be depression. Nothing about my life feels like it's a second chance. I'm a one-armed author who's lost his muse. I don't know where she is or even if she's okay.

All I know is that this doesn't feel like anything I can handle.

Nearly forty minutes later, Albert calls back with the information I've been waiting for. "She's at a friend's house in Dutchess County. Some woman named Sienna Rollins. Do you know the name?"

"No. Maybe. I don't know. Who is she?" I ask, feeling like I do know the name but not sure if too much Netflix has finally totally fucked up my head.

"She's an actress. All I know about her is she divorced some billionaire businessman a couple years ago and made out like a bandit. Other than that, I only have the address of her house upstate."

He gives it to me and I write it down on a scrap of paper I immediately slip into my pocket. The address is tattooed onto my brain. It's where Kristina is, so that's where I need to be.

I DRIVE UP to Sienna Rollins' multi-million dollar property in Verbank, New York and can't help but be impressed. I may never have heard of her name or seen any of her films, but she's clearly done well for herself. Not that I care about any of that.

All I care about is finding Kristina.

A middle-aged woman in a grey and white maid's uniform answers the door and after I give her my name, she ushers me into an enormous two story white foyer, instructing me to wait until she gets Mrs. Rollins. As I stand there, my stomach feels like someone's twisting it into knots as question after question forms in my mind. Why didn't Kristina tell me where she was all this time? Not one phone call in months doesn't sound like her. She's alive, but did something happen to change her feelings for me? Or did she think I died?

A tall, shapely woman with long blond hair appears in front of me in jeans and a sweatshirt as I wonder what happened to Kristina and gives me a smile that I sense is forced. A beautiful woman, she seems out of place there surrounded by all this obvious wealth.

"Mr. Anwell, I'm Sienna Rollins. What can I do for you?"

"Please call me Ian. I'm here to see Kristina. I know she's here, and I need to speak to her."

Sienna's eyes open wide, like she's surprised at what I've just said, and for a moment that forced smile fades a little. It reappears just seconds later, though, as she says, "Ian, it's very nice to meet you. I'll have to see if Kristina wants any visitors."

"Why is she here? It's been nearly five months since the accident. Does she know I'm okay? Why didn't she try to see me?"

Reaching out, Sienna takes my hand and gives it a sympathetic squeeze. "I'm probably not the right person to ask. I'll find out if Kristina can see you."

She leaves me standing there in that white foyer as my stomach continues to churn over all those questions I have. All I want is to see the woman I love and who loves me. If Sienna knows Kristina at all, she knows about me. Why wouldn't she immediately take me to see her?

I hear footsteps and see Sienna walking toward me from down a long hallway. I can tell by the look on her face that the answer is no, that

I can't see Kristina. But why?

"Kristina can't see you today, Ian. Maybe another day. Let me take your number and she can call you."

"No. I want answers and I want them now. Why is she here and not back at her apartment in the city? Why wouldn't she want to see me? Why in all the time I was in the hospital didn't she even try to visit me or find out if I was okay? What's going on here?"

"I don't want to upset you, Ian. I'm really not trying to do that. I just need you to understand now isn't a good time."

"Why? What's going on with her? We left my cabin that morning happily in love and ready to move in together, and now you tell me she doesn't want to see me. I want to know why."

Sienna looks away and I consider pushing past her to find Kristina on my own, but then she turns back and says, "Come with me. Let me explain."

Leading me into an opulently decorated living room at the front of the house, she extends her arm to offer me a seat on a large white sofa. We sit down next to one another, and I wait for her to begin explaining what the hell is going on. After what seems like an eternity, she takes a deep breath and begins speaking.

"I'm sorry things have turned out so badly for you two. Kristina loved you. I want you to know that. That day of the accident, she went over that embankment too, ending up at the bottom of that ravine with you. Thankfully, her injuries weren't life threatening, but that didn't mean they weren't serious. She went through the windshield, Ian, so her injuries occurred mostly on her face."

She stops talking and a frown settles into her mouth. I know what the problem is now. "Sienna, I don't care what she looks like. I love her. Her outside doesn't matter to me."

"It matters to her, Ian. She was an actress on the verge of hitting it big, and now she feels like she's lost everything in that part of her life. I know it's only been a short time and with plastic surgery she can someday be like she was before, but she doesn't believe that. She sees herself as that person who she sees in the mirror every day. The cuts have healed, but the scars remain."

"I understand, but we can get past that. All I need is some time with her."

"It's more than that. She blames herself for the accident. She knows what happened to you. I found out and told her, and she was horrified. She thinks she's ruined your life."

I look down at my left arm and the useless hand that dangles at the end of it before I look back at Sienna. "It wasn't her fault. She did nothing to cause that accident. Just let me see her and I can explain all that to her. My life isn't ruined. I'm still here, just with one less hand I can use."

"Her emotional injuries are why she doesn't want to see you, Ian. She's just not ready, I guess. I don't know when she's going to be ready either. Most days she just sits in her room and reads her books. Your books."

"I need to see her, Sienna. I'm not leaving until I get to see her."

She shakes her head and frowns. "I can't do that, Ian. She's not ready."

CHAPTER TEN

Kristina

THE LIGHT COMING through the window seems so bright today, and I close the curtains to block some of it out. I catch a glimpse of my reflection in the window and cringe, hating the monster that looks back at me. That woman isn't Kristina Richards. She can't be.

A part of me wants to run out to stop Sienna from sending Ian away. After all these months of being without him, just knowing he's so close makes me need him as much as ever, but I can't. Not looking like this.

I was his muse, the woman he became obsessed with after seeing my movies. The woman whose looks inspired him to write. How can I face him now looking like this? Who would want a damaged muse?

My fingertips trace the scars from my right eye and down my cheek to my jawline. Raised pink lines that make me look like a hideous stranger even to myself. How could I expect him to ever look at me the same way? I don't look like the person he fell in love with anymore.

I sit down in my chair again and hold his book to my heart, the only piece of him I have left now. Opening the cover, I turn the page to where he signed his name to his biggest fan and trace my fingertip over the sharp lines of his signature.

Does he even write now after the accident? The day Sienna finally told me about his injury flashes through my mind, as does the pain of knowing how much his loss means to him. If only I hadn't distracted him as we drove down that snowy mountain road. If only that truck hadn't come around the corner so wide. If only we'd stayed at the cabin another day or another hour. If only we'd stayed in bed for just a few minutes more, none of this would have happened.

As always, everything about us revolves around if onlys.

I wanted to tell Sienna nothing would make me happier than to see Ian again, but how can face him like this? It's better this way. He'll find another muse who will inspire him to write again.

My chest aches at the idea of another woman being that for him. Like my heart wants to believe we can be like we were again, but one glance at my reflection in the window and my brain tells my heart the awful truth.

The sound of his voice hits me like a bolt of lightning, and I listen as he demands to see me, even as Sienna tells him it's not possible. Then I hear footsteps coming down the hallway, and panic tears through me. He's coming to see me, but he can't. I can't see him like this!

Just as I reach out to lock the door, it opens and there he is. I cover my face with my hands and turn away from him, unable to even look him in the eye. "Go away, Ian. You shouldn't be here. Please go."

"No. I came here to see you, and I'm not leaving until you talk to me. I don't care if your friend calls the police and they have to drag me out of here. I need to know the answers to my questions."

"Please go. I don't have the answers you want."

I hear him walk toward me, and then his hand touches my shoulder and it's like we've never been apart. All the feelings I've tried so hard to push down deep inside so he can move on rush back to the surface, making it impossible to hold back the tears.

"I'm not going anywhere. I know about what happened to you, and it doesn't matter what you look like. I'm not the same after the accident either. It doesn't matter. Nothing matters more than I love you, Kristina."

"It does matter, Ian. Please just leave me here to live my life hidden away."

He wraps his arm around me and kisses the top of my head. "You don't have to hide. Come home with me like we planned at the cabin and be my muse again."

I can't control my sobs as they wash over me at the thought of being his muse once more. As Ian holds me to him, I whisper the truth. "I can never be your muse again. The accident made sure of that. Please just leave and let me be."

"You don't want that. I can't believe you don't love me anymore, Kristina. No matter what's happened, you're still my muse just like I'm still a writer, even though I only have one working hand. Nothing's changed."

Pulling away from him, I throw myself on the bed and hide my face in the pillow so he can't see just how wrong he is. Everything's changed. My looks are gone, just like the use of his hand, because of me. How he could want to see me again I can't understand, but even if he's willing to forgive me, it doesn't matter.

What we were can never be again.

I feel his hand caressing my back, and my body reacts like it always has to his touch. I wish I could face him so he could take me in his arms and hold me until all the bad goes away. I've missed him so much.

"Kristina, please listen to me. I know what happened to you, but I don't love you because of your outside. I love the woman you are on the inside. The way you make me a better man than I've ever been before. Your strength when I didn't have any. You stuck around when I needed you. Now I'm here when you need me."

"It's not the same, Ian. I'm not the same. Everything I was is gone. That Kristina Richards died in that accident."

"Then we have a chance to start over again. We wanted to take that chance that day. Do you remember? We were going to go back to the city and start our life together. We can still do that."

I shake my head in the pillow. "No, we can't. I can't be your muse anymore."

Ian lies down next to me and presses his lips to my ear to whisper, "Then don't be. I don't need you to be my muse. I need you to be the woman I love. Please look at me. Trust me, Kristina."

"No. I can't. I'm not that person anymore."

"And I'm not the man you fell in love with either. I'm an author who has to handwrite his books now, but I still love you the same way I did before."

Ian's mention of his injured arm only makes me cry more. I did that. I caused him to lose the ability to use his arm. "I never meant for any of this to happen. I swear, Ian. I'm so sorry."

His hand brushes the hair from the good side of my face, and he gently kisses me on my cheek. "You didn't do this to me. This happened because a truck made a wide turn and caused an accident. No one meant for any of this to happen. It just happened. But we can get past this. If you can overlook my changes, I know I can see past yours. We aren't an arm or a few scars. Tell me you know we're more than that. Tell me you remember what we were and can be again if you just give us a chance."

"No. I can't. Everything I was is gone now. I can't bear the idea of seeing what I was in your eyes when you look at me."

He's silent for so long even as he stays there next to me that I know what I feared is true. I don't blame him. He fell in love with a woman who had beauty, and now that she doesn't, he shouldn't have to stay when he doesn't want to.

"I'm sorry, Kristina. I'm sorry for making you think that I fell in love with you because of how you look. I never meant to let you think that's all you were to me."

"I was your muse, Ian. Now what am I? You don't have to say you love me because you feel bad. You never signed on to be with a woman who looks like this."

Ian kisses me again and in a voice full of pain says, "Please look at me, Kristina. Show me you still love me like I love you."

"I can't," I sob, wishing more than anything I didn't look like I do. "I can't bear to see your reaction knowing you loved how I looked."

The bed moves as he rolls away from me, and I sense he's finally given up. I don't blame him. Some things are just too much to overcome. But then just as I think he's about to leave, he sits down next to me on the side my scars are on and out of the corner of my eye I see him lift his left coat sleeve to show me his arm.

"Do you know that even though I lost the use of my arm in that accident, my biggest fear as I drove up here was that you didn't want me anymore because I'm always going to be a recovering addict?"

I hear in his words the truth he always lives with, and I can't let him think that. Turning to face him with my scarred cheek still covered by my hair, I say, "I loved you knowing who you were all along. You never lied to me about that, so I had no reason to not want you. But this isn't the same, Ian."

"I don't know what to say to make you understand I don't care what your outside looks like. What kind of writer am I who can't find the words to convince the woman I love to believe me?"

"You're a wonderful writer. Don't say that."

"I can't be that wonderful if I can't even tell you what you need to hear to trust me."

He deserves better than to think he's lacking because I am, so I muster all the courage I have inside me and slowly sit up next to him. I hang my head so my hair covers my ugliness, but his fingers gently tuck it behind my ear so my scars and everything I am now is on full display. Squeezing my eyes shut, I close them tightly to avoid the look in his eyes as he sees me for the first time.

"Look at me, please. Please, Kristina."

I shake my head and whisper, "No. I can't face you like this."

"Please, Kristina."

I can't say no, even though I wish I could, and I finally face the fear that's haunted me from the first time I saw myself after the accident. Slowly, I open my eyes to see him staring at me with that same look of love in his dark eyes that's always made me feel so adored and wanted.

With his fingertip, he caresses my cheek, touching each of my scars as he looks into my eyes. "I missed you so much, my beautiful Kristina. Please don't make me live without you anymore. Come home so we can begin the life we planned."

"I can't be an actress anymore because of how I look. What am I going to do with my life now?"

Ian leans over and kisses my damaged cheek. "I know an author who desperately needs someone to help him write. How does co-author sound?"

"Co-author? On what?"

"Silk and Steel, our story. We lived it, so you might as well get the credit too. We'll write it together." He lifts his left arm and smiles. "Of course, you'll have to do the typing since I'm pretty slow these days."

"Me, a co-author? I'm not a writer, Ian."

His mouth turns down into a frown. "Come with me anyway. Please. Don't give up on us now."

I think about all we've been through and look into his eyes still so full of love for me, even though I'm not the woman he fell in love with, and I can't say no to him. Cradling his face, I say the truest words I've spoken in months. "I don't want to give up on us, Ian. I want to go home."

His smile lights up his whole face, and he takes me into his arms. "I promise you won't regret this, Kristina. I love you."

I feel his heartbeat against my cheek and for the first time in months, I feel like I'm already home again.

✧　✧　✧

IAN PRACTICALLY LEVITATES off the couch with excitement next to me as the credits roll on the HBO production of Silk. I know he's dying to hear my opinion on it, but to tease him I pretend to have to consider the answer to his question how I liked the film.

"Well? What did you think?"

"I can see why you kept it from me even when they gave you a copy to preview," I say as I turn to face him.

He's unable to keep his disappointment hidden. Crestfallen, he mumbles, "You didn't like it?"

I've tortured him enough, so I smile and throw my arms around him. "I love it! I wasn't sure how I'd feel since I always wanted to play the part of Kate, but it's wonderful, Ian."

He backs away from me and smiles from ear to ear. "I knew you'd love it. The parts the screenwriter added fit so well I can't say I'd have done better if I did it myself. I'm so happy you loved it as much as I do. They really brought Kate and Sean to life."

It's been three long years since I convinced

him that the film should be made even though I couldn't play the role of Kate. We've grown stronger since the accident, and although his left arm still doesn't work and my scars are still visible in certain light even after my plastic surgery, we're as much in love as we've ever been. We still love completely and madly, and when we fight, it's with the same passion as we love. I adore him as much as he adores me, but those two damaged souls we were when we met are still inside us, demons lying in wait for a time when we're weak and they can strike again.

But after what we've been through, we're both strong. Him for me and me for him. So those addictions and obsessions that are so much a part of each of us no longer rule our life together.

Cradling his face, I kiss his lips and smile. "I don't care what critics think or anyone else. I love it because it's the story of us. And I know that it's not just our story anymore, but in my heart it will always be just you and me, Ian."

As he takes me into his arms and holds me close, he corrects me about Silk as he always has. "It was you, Kristina. Always you."

CONTINUE READING FOR INFORMATION ON MORE OF KM'S BOOKS AND FIND YOUR NEXT GREAT READ!

IF I DREAM (CORRUPTED LOVE #1)

A story of passion, crime, and the lengths you go to for love…

If I dream, will you dare?

Ryder
All I wanted was my freedom. It's all I'd dreamed of from the first time I stood in the ring. Until I entered Robert Erickson's world. Until Serena. Cruelty and ugliness surrounded me, but she was beautiful and good. I wanted to protect her from her father's world, even though I knew being with her could mean the end of me.

Serena
I wanted for nothing as the daughter of one of the richest men in the world. But all my father's money couldn't buy what I truly craved. Until Ryder. I wanted all he was, all he brought out in me. All he made me desire.

Our love was forbidden by the one person who had the power to harm us. We dreamed of more than living in that world, though. We dreamed of having it all, but did we dare?

CHAPTER ONE

Ryder

AS USUAL, THE crowd at The Pit screamed its lust for the two of us to pound the fuck out of each other. Impatient bastards. I couldn't hear any one person's words clearly, but I'd done this enough times to know what the people who'd come to watch us wanted.

Blood. Pain. And one of us as close to death as possible. It thrilled them in some sick way almost as much as I suspected winning did when their fighter crushed another person.

My opponent tonight stood nearly as tall as I did at six foot three, but his body was smaller than mine. He looked older, like something in the way he carried himself said he'd seen more of life than I had. His angular face looked hard, and on either side of his perfectly straight nose were eyes staring me down like he thought squinting and grimacing would make me run for the nearest exit like some fucking scared little boy. He was fighting the wrong person if that's what he expected.

I'd never lost and for good reason. When you had nothing but the feel of your fists beating the hell out of someone and the sound of those rabid fucks cheering you on like you were some kind of hero for nearly killing another man, all you wanted was to win.

Fifteen times I'd won right here in this dank warehouse against guys bigger and stronger than me, and every time it seemed to surprise everyone. Even those who had bet on me.

If they only knew how unlikely it was anyone could match the rage inside me, they'd never bet against me again.

Some impatient bastard behind me barked, "Stop dancing around! Hit 'em!"

Mr. Grimace narrowed his eyes until he could barely see out of them and took a deep breath. Why did he bother with all this tough guy bullshit? That's not what these bloodthirsty fucks wanted.

Pain is what they wanted.

So that's what they'd get. His or mine. It didn't matter to them.

"Scared, motherfucker?" he grunted out in a deep voice I knew wasn't really how he talked. "I'm going to fuck you up."

I didn't bother answering.

He caught me in the face with a hard right that scrambled my brains for a second, and then his fist skidded along my jaw and ran square into my right shoulder. The last guy I fought had done a number on that one, so that hurt like a bitch.

I knew how this went, though. The people around us wanted a show as much as they wanted a fight. I could have just beat the fuck out of him and won, but that's not what this was. I'd been told that enough times to understand even if I could pound the piss out of a guy, I had to at least make it look like a fight and not just some sad beat down.

So that's what I did. I took a few hits, sometimes more than a few, and let it look like there was some chance I wouldn't win. The other guy got to feel pretty big in the shorts and the crowd got to feel like this was really a match between two fighters.

It wasn't, though.

He paraded around like a peacock, preening to the crowd while I gritted my teeth and pushed my shoulder back into place. I took a deep breath and waited for the moment I'd show him who he was dealing with.

Flush with the love of the crowd, he turned back to face me. A few shots into me had made him think he had a chance.

I stepped forward as he lunged at me and leveled my fist against his jaw. His head ricocheted back, sending him reeling for a second or two, but I didn't let up. My right hand zeroed in on his face again, this time connecting with his cheekbone. I felt it crack against my knuckles bulging out of my fist and saw him stagger back away from me.

But he would get no mercy from me. That wasn't what I was here for.

"Get him!" the crowd screamed as the guy cowered, hanging his head to protect his busted face.

That wouldn't help him, though. Not with me. I knew what my role was. I knew why all these people had come here tonight, and it wasn't to see mercy. Mercy was for suckers. Fuck mercy.

They wanted blood and pain, and blood and pain is what they'd get.

I walked toward him as a feeling of complete calm came over me. All the noise of the crowd around us faded away until all I heard were the words I told myself every time I stood to fight.

It's you or him. Nothing more. Either you win or he does, but if you lose, you'll have nothing.

He looked up and I saw the pleading in his eyes. I'd seen it fifteen times before. No matter how big and tough they'd been in the beginning, each one ended up giving me that same sad look that said they wanted me to be someone other than who they'd heard I was.

Someone other than who I had to be.

Maybe they fought for some reason that had nothing to do with their very survival. Maybe they thought it would be fun, or it would make them feel tough. Maybe they thought they had something to prove to some girl. Whatever their reasons for agreeing to fight, they weren't why I fought.

For me, every win put me one step closer to being free. I didn't fight for shits and giggles or because I wanted to impress some skirt. I fought for the chance that one day I would never have to step foot in this fucking shithole place again. I fought because deep in the back of my mind there existed the tiniest dream that one day I'd be normal and have a normal life.

That one day I wouldn't have to be the man I'd been forced to become in this fight.

I knew his weak spots and attacked them. My fists pummeled his face, and no matter how hard he tried to shield himself from the blows, it was no use. Over and over, I hit him until that pretty face of his looked like mangled hamburger. Blood, flesh, and bone mixed to make a horror show. The nose that had been so straight just a few minutes before now pointed down toward his mouth like some deranged compass.

As I stood up to my full height, I heard the crowd cheering, as if I'd done something worthy of praise. A man lay in a crumpled heap at my feet, defeated and broken, and these fuckers were thrilled about it.

Looking around, I saw some clapping and others pumping their fists in the air as my win filled them with some kind of messed up happiness. Who was I kidding? What it filled was their wallets. That's why they were so happy.

Floyd raised my right arm in the air to the delight of the rabid fans and said in my ear, "That's my boy. You done good, son."

I forced a smile and nodded my head. I wasn't his boy and he wasn't my father. I was his fighter and he was the scumbag who went out to find people for me to fight. Whatever else he thought we were was all in his mind.

He lowered my arm and slapped me on the back. "Go relax. You deserve it. You put on a good show. Just look at the way these people love you!"

I tore my stare from his greasy comb-over and beady eyes and looked over his head to see the people who loved me. Between the booze, the drugs, and the fight, they looked like wild animals.

Who was worse? Them or me?

"RYDER, THERE'S SOMEONE here to talk to you," Floyd yelled from the other side of the door.

I didn't want to talk to anyone. All I wanted to do was sit on my crappy metal folding chair in this dingy room and hope my shoulder started feeling better. I'd downed a few shots of Floyd's whisky about ten minutes ago, but so far, it hadn't helped ease the pain.

"Not now," I yelled back.

He'd only open the door anyway. I knew that. It still felt good to let him and whoever the hell was standing there with him know that I didn't want to talk.

The door opened a second later and I saw Floyd and some guy who looked far too well-dressed to be anywhere near the warehouse on any night standing in my shitty little room. He had a vibe that screamed money with his suit, expensive shoes, and slicked back grey hair that made him look what my mother used to call stately.

"This is Mr. Robert Erickson," Floyd said as the man walked into the room like he owned the place. "I'll leave you two to talk."

I'd never seen Floyd leave a scene that fast. As he closed the door, I looked at the man who stood in front of me and saw he was studying me as much as I was him. Not that I was all too curious about what he wanted. People dressed like he was coming into my world never brought anything good with them.

Never.

The intruder looked around the cinder block room I called mine and then looked down at me. "Ryder, as our mutual friend Floyd said, my name is Robert Erickson. Do you know who I am?"

Shaking my head, I shrugged. "Nope. Should I?"

His dark eyebrows drew in like angry black slashes and his eyes narrowed to slits, much like the way the guy I just beat to a pulp had looked at the beginning of our fight. "I'm the man who runs this show. You are sitting in my warehouse and fighting in my stable. So yes, maybe you should know who I am."

As much as I knew he thought I should be impressed by this, I wasn't. Folding my arms across my chest, I said, "Oh yeah? Nice to meet the big boss then. I hope you bet on me tonight."

His eyes opened wider as the corners of his mouth inched up into what reminded me of how a crocodile looked right before he ate his prey. "You're pretty sure of yourself, aren't you?"

I looked up at the ceiling for a moment,

unsure how I should answer that. Fuck yeah, I was sure of myself. I may not have been wearing a thousand dollar suit and fine leather shoes like him, but I had gifts of my own that had made me a winner sixteen times already.

Pursing my lips, I shrugged again. "I haven't lost yet. Come see me when I do and I'll tell you how cocky I'm feeling then."

His crocodile smile spread even wider across his face. Nodding, he said, "I'll remember that. For now, I'm here to tell you I've bought your contract from Floyd. So now you work for only me."

The words hit me like a fist to the face. I didn't have a contract with Floyd or anyone else. I fought to pay off money I owed him, and when that debt was paid off, I'd get to leave this shithole world of fighting. Now all that seemed like a pipe dream this fucker had dashed to pieces.

I stood from my rusted metal chair and stared at Robert Erickson. "What does that mean?"

Nearly the same height, he met my gaze with one so intense I thought about taking a step back. When he spoke, it sounded like his voice came from somewhere dark.

"It means I own you now. You fight for me and I expect you to win like you always have."

Left unsaid was the implicit threat that hung

off every word. If you lose, you'll suffer. The only question was how.

My mind spun at the news that all I'd planned, all I'd worked for, was gone now. "So I guess my deal with Floyd to be released from fighting when I paid off what I owed him is gone too?"

"Yes."

"And if I don't agree to this new deal?" I asked, silently gauging my chances of not only getting past him but finding some way of surviving after I got away. He was big, and I had a sneaking suspicion even bigger guys stood outside waiting for him.

Robert Erickson looked like the type of man who got what he wanted, one way or another, whether the other person involved wanted it or not.

"You have no say in it, but let me assure you that you want to fight for me. For now, let's get you to your place so you can pack your things."

He turned to open the door as I explained this room was my place. "No need to go anywhere. You're already in it."

Erickson slowly looked back at me with confusion written all over his face. "You live here?"

I nodded. "Yeah. Short commute time to

work and everything I need within arm's reach. What more could a guy ask for?"

Closing the door, he turned to face me. "How old are you?"

"Eighteen."

"And you live here, in my warehouse where Floyd holds fights for me?" he asked as he looked around my room again, this time with a look of disgust like the fact made him sick.

"Yep. Better than the street or jail. I might not get three hots, but I got a cot and a shower."

My answer didn't make the sickened expression leave his face, but he nodded anyway. "Well, gather your things. It's time to go."

I opened my mouth to ask where, but he walked out and left me standing there in that room I'd lived in for the past three months. As I stuffed the few clothes I owned, deodorant, and my toothbrush into a duffel bag, I thought wherever I was going had to be better than this place.

WE PULLED UP to a massive black gate between two even bigger rows of hedges and stopped momentarily as the driver got the go ahead to drive onto the property. I couldn't help but stare out the window as we drove up the long driveway past some kind of fountain that looked like something the Greek gods might swim in and a bunch of smaller hedges than the ones out front that looked like the gardener had cut them all into bird shapes. Robert Erickson was even richer than I'd first thought. Only insanely wealthy people lived in places like this.

The car stopped in front of a house so big I couldn't see all of it as I looked out the car window. Erickson tapped me on the arm as I stared out at the mansion and said, "Welcome home."

Home? This couldn't be my home. Instantly, the thought of what I'd have to do to live in a place like this raced through my mind. Fighting in The Pit wasn't going to be enough to live in a house like the one I saw in front of me.

I opened the car door and stepped out onto a stone driveway as I gaped at the house, which was even more impressive without the tinting of the car window getting in my way. Huge white columns towered above us to the second story of the gold colored home, and a glass front door so enormous I'd never seen one so big stood behind them.

"Follow me," was all Erickson said as he led the way to those doors. I couldn't imagine what waited inside after an outside this incredible.

I did as he ordered and caught up to him as he

walked into an entryway so big the sound of our shoes hitting the white marble tile on the floor echoed off the matching marble tiled walls. He strode through like nothing around us was special toward the most spectacular curved wrought iron staircase I'd ever seen.

Not that I had seen many curved staircases with wrought iron in my life. I think I'd seen either a grand total of two times in a magazine some girl had in English class one time. I really didn't have much interest in reading architectural magazines, but she did and since I wanted to get in her pants, I sat next to her after school as she told me all about her dreams of having a huge house with a curved staircase and a wrought iron railing one day.

She would have loved Erickson's place. For me, it made me feel small, something very few people or things had achieved in a long time. Not small, actually. More like insignificant.

As my head swiveled left and right to look at the artwork on the walls, Robert said, "Come in here to my office. I want you to meet some people."

My hand clutched the handle of my duffel bag tightly in my palm. Meet some people? I didn't even look like they'd let me on the property to be the goddamned gardener who made hedges into animal shapes and now he wanted to introduce me to some people?

That feeling of insignificance morphed into one of pure discomfort. I didn't belong there, no matter how much he wanted to parade me through the place, and whoever he wanted me to meet would know that as sure as I did.

He led me into his office, a room even bigger than the entryway and as dark as that was light. This room had dark green walls the color of a pool table and a dark wood floor. Floor to ceiling bookcases held books with names I'd never heard of and sculptures I guessed cost more than my life was worth.

"Wait here. I'll be right back," he announced before leaving as I continued to look around in awe.

Seconds later, he came back with two females and ordered them into his office. Neither one looked like him, but something about the way they acted told me they weren't servants or people he'd just basically bought, like me.

They stopped dead at the sight of me standing there in my old gym pants and black t-shirt and the one I figured was older spun around to look at him in disgust.

"Who is this?"

"Girls, this is Ryder. He's going to be living

here, so treat him like family."

Robert's proclamation infuriated her, and she shook her head angrily. "What, like a brother? You go out one night and get us a brother? Is that how it goes, Dad?"

He ignored her outburst and turned his two daughters to face me. "Ryder, the one who can't stop talking is Janelle. The other one is Serena."

"Hi," I mumbled, unsure if I should say anything.

They both stood staring at me like I was some foreign thing that needed to be removed and fast. The one named Janelle had short dark brown hair, and although I couldn't be sure since her eyes were flashing so much hatred, I thought they were brown too. Thin, she wore jeans and a tight blue shirt and heels that gave her at least three inches on her normal height.

The other one, Serena, had lighter brown hair that fell to below her shoulders in soft waves that reminded me of what mermaids looked like. Dressed in jean shorts and a white t-shirt that both showed off her tan and toned body, she stood barefoot next to her father and stared at me with big brown eyes that didn't have hatred but something else in them.

Disappointment?

As Janelle returned to complaining about my

very existence, I heard Serena say in a pained voice, "You said you knew where she was. You promised you'd find her this time. Where is she?"

I imagined that's what that guy with the pleading eyes would have sounded like if he begged me not to beat the shit out of him. The way she said those words made my chest hurt, and I didn't even know who she was talking about.

But Robert was unmoved by her pleading. Waving off her questions, he said, "Maybe next time, honey. For now, I want you two to welcome Ryder to our home."

He put his arms around both of them, but Janelle slipped out of his hold and stormed off without another word. I didn't have to guess how she felt about me. Serena said nothing more about what was obviously so important to her and simply looked at me with that pleading in her eyes that hadn't worked on her father.

With a nudge from him, she finally said, "Welcome to our home. I hope you like it here."

And with that, she quietly left without another word to her father about whoever she wanted him to find.

Robert walked behind his desk and sat down in his chair as I watched her walk away, her sagging shoulders signaling how defeated she felt. Clearly, it didn't affect her father at all.

"They'll get used to you. Janelle is a little temperamental, but I guess that's to be expected from a girl, even one her age. She's a lot like me, though, so at least she has that going for her. Serena is the polar opposite. She's like her mother. Don't worry about her. She'll take to you like every stray she brings home."

Not that I didn't know I looked like some stray dog compared to them, but the way he said it brought the reality home for sure. In a hurry to get out of there and to wherever he kept the strays he brought home, I said, "Well, if you can just point me in the direction of where you want me to go, I'll get out of your hair."

He shook his head as that crocodile smile spread across his face again. "Not yet. First, I want you to know what I expect of you. So sit down and relax."

Dropping my duffel bag, I sat down in a chair in front of his desk as he'd ordered and listened to hear just what this whole arrangement would involve.

He steepled his fingers in front of him and began. "You'll continue to fight as you did tonight. As I said before, I expect you to continue to win. When you do, you'll get paid, despite the fact that you won't need money as long as you live here."

"I won't need money?" I asked, confused what kind of world this guy lived in that didn't require cash.

Lifting his chin, he shook his head. "No, you won't. Your room and board, along with all the food you want and clothes you need, will be provided. I have a state of the art workout center you're to use to make sure you're in the best shape possible. So you see, you won't need money."

I didn't know if I should question this whole situation that sounded too good to be true, but I asked, "And if I don't win a fight?"

His face grew dark. "Let's cross that bridge when we come to it. For now, I have very few rules, other than you performing in fights like I've seen. No drugs and no romantic attachments. I don't care who you fuck, but don't get involved. I remember being your age, so I don't expect you to live like a monk, but no relationships."

I wasn't a fan of having so much of my life dictated, but assuming I got a room even as big as a broom closet on his estate, maybe it wouldn't be too much of a tradeoff. I wasn't exactly looking for a relationship anyway and I didn't do drugs. Hoping he wasn't about to announce that I had to double as a stable boy or something like that, I smiled.

"Okay. I can live with those."

"And you aren't to tell anyone here what you do. Is that clear?"

"Sure. But if I'm not here as a fighter, what am I supposed to say if someone asks?"

"They won't," he said with a confidence I guessed came from being the boss.

"Got it."

"Good. I'll have my housekeeper take you to your room. For now, you'll have the spare bedroom on this floor."

A short, dark haired woman he called Josephine appeared a few seconds later, so I stood from my chair and grabbed my duffel bag to go with her. I felt like there were a lot more questions I should ask Robert, but he didn't seem interested in talking anymore and picked up the phone to call someone, so I smiled again and moved to leave.

Just before I reached the door, he said, "Oh, Ryder, one more thing."

There it was. The one thing that would make this whole situation unbearable. I slowly turned around and waited for the other shoe to drop.

"Don't even think of doing anything with either of the girls. In that respect, I do care who you fuck."

I thought back to how much Janelle hated me already and easily put the idea of fucking her out of my mind. And Serena? I wasn't sure if she was even legal, and I didn't need that dogging me. An angry father was one thing, but prison was an entirely different story.

She was beautiful, though. There was something about her I could definitely like, if things were different. But no matter how beautiful she was, I wasn't touching that.

"No problem," I answered with confidence, hoping that was the worst thing about living at Erickson's house.

If it was, this would be the best thing to ever happen to me, even if it meant I had to keep fighting. Maybe freedom wasn't all it was cracked up to be anyway.

LOOK FOR THE CORRUPTED LOVE TRILOGY TODAY!
AVAILABLE AT ALL MAJOR RETAILERS

About the Author

K.M. Scott writes contemporary romance stories of sexy, intense, and unforgettable love. A New York Times and USA Today bestselling author, she's been in love with romance since reading her first romance novel in junior high (she was a very curious girl!). Under her Gabrielle Bisset name, she writes erotic paranormal and historical romance. She lives in Pennsylvania with a herd of animals and when she's not writing can be found reading or feeding her TV addiction.

Be sure to visit K.M.'s Facebook page at **facebook.com/kmscottauthor** for all the latest on her books, along with giveaways and other goodies! And to hear all the news on K.M. Scott books first, sign up for her newsletter today and be sure to visit her website at **www.kmscottbooks.com**.

Books by K.M. Scott:

If I Dream (Corrupted Love #1)
If You Fight (Corrupted Love #2)
If We Fall (Corrupted Love #3)

Crash Into Me (Heart of Stone #1)
Fall Into Me (Heart of Stone #2)
Give In To Me (Heart of Stone #3)
Heart of Stone Volume One Box Set
Ever After (Heart of Stone #4)
A Heart of Stone Christmas (Heart of Stone #5)
Unforgettable (Heart of Stone #6)
Unbreakable (Heart of Stone #7)
Heart of Stone Volume Two Box Set

Temptation (Club X #1)
Surrender (Club X #2)
Possession (Club X #3)
Satisfaction (Club X #4)
Acceptance (Club X #5)
The Complete Club X Series Box Set

Crave (Addicted To You #1)
Adore (Addicted To You #2)
Shatter (Addicted To You #3)
Claim (Addicted To You #4)

K.M.'S BOOKS ARE IN AUDIOBOOK TOO!

Books by Gabrielle Bisset:

Vampire Dreams Revamped (A Sons of Navarus Prequel)
Blood Avenged (Sons of Navarus #1)
Blood Betrayed (Sons of Navarus #2)
Longing (A Sons of Navarus Short Story)
Blood Spirit (Sons of Navarus #3)
The Deepest Cut (A Sons of Navarus Short Story)
Blood Prophecy (Sons of Navarus #4)
Blood Craving (Sons of Navarus #5)
Blood Eclipse (Sons of Navarus #6)
The Sons of Navarus Box Set #1
The Sons of Navarus Box Set #2

Stolen Destiny (Destined Ones Duology #1)
Destiny Redeemed (Destined Ones Duology #2)

Love's Master
Masquerade
The Victorian Erotic Romance Trilogy

www.ingramcontent.com/pod-product-compliance
Lightning Source LLC
Chambersburg PA
CBHW032032180726
48284CB00008B/2562